"I'll have you begging yet, Jericho."

Kate issued the declaration with a tight, sexy grin on her lips, before she made it crystal clear. "I'll win, Jericho. I always do." She adjusted her low-cut collar and shimmied in her gauzy skirt as she left her lab table.

Jericho's easy grin quickly became serious looking as he reached out and captured her hand. Turning it over, he gently caressed her palm. "What makes you think you won't give in first?"

"Pure determination." Kate paused, staring right at Jericho. "It's mind over matter. And I'm very good at that. What are you good at?" She threw the words at him.

"Making you scream out in gut-clenching, heart-stopping pleasure."

"Good answer," Kate said, her eyes widening as Jericho stood and looked deep into her eyes and took her mouth in a searing earth-shattering kiss.

Dear Reader,

You hold the last book of my first mini-series, WOMEN WHO DARE, in your hands. It was a wonderful ride. Now, in *Mine to Entice*, Kate gets her chance to show everyone that she's no longer "Sister Kate." She entices Jericho into her bed and he releases the wild woman in her. But what happens when that woman is set free and she wants so much more than just a souvenir from Jericho?

I hope you enjoyed this journey with me as much as I did creating it. Thanks for being a Woman Who Dares and for picking up my series. I love to hear from readers, so please contact me at www.karenanders.com

Best!

Karen Anders

MINE TO ENTICE

by

Karen Anders

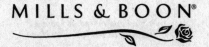

MILLS & BOON®

To Kathryn Lye for believing in me and giving me the freedom to create.

A special thanks to Dr Dan Krane from Forensic Bioinformatics, Inc for
his generosity and his invaluable DNA guidance. All mistakes are mine.

*First published in Great Britain 2005
by Harlequin Mills & Boon Limited,
Eton House, 18-24 Paradise Road, Richmond, Surrey TW9 1SR*

© Karen Alarie 2004

ISBN 0 263 84454 4

14-0405

*Printed and bound in Spain
by Litografia Rosés S.A., Barcelona*

1

WHERE THE HELL was Kate? Jericho St. James thought to himself as he continued with the questioning of his next-to-last witness. He'd scheduled Kate Quinn last for the impact of her testimony, but she hadn't come in on time. He had no idea if she was waiting outside the courtroom…or not. He couldn't even ask the judge if he could skip over her, since she *was* the only witness he had left.

Just as he asked his final question, he nodded to the bailiff who knew to go get Kate. Hopefully she was sitting just outside the door.

He opened his mouth to tell the judge he had no more questions, but the courtroom doors opened and Kate walked through.

Jericho stared. He couldn't help it. He'd never seen buttoned-up Kate Quinn dressed this way. It wasn't as if the dress was too tight or too sexy. It was conservative and covered all the important parts. It was the whole package that had him gaping.

It was true that he found it very difficult to concentrate when Kate was in the room, no matter how she was dressed. She looked like innocence person-ified, wide open and defenseless and soft, like whipped cream, like butter, like silk. But there was something about her that promised ecstasy and fire, something that was inherent, but dormant.

Heat infused every pore of his body with the sight of her loose, untamed head of curly blond hair fram-ing her arresting face, sliding and dipping over her delicate shoulders, disappearing down her back. He'd imagined plenty of times how it would look down, feel against his skin, clenched in his fist. It was like cornsilk, glossy and beautiful.

And the dress she wore. Damn.

The color of passion flowed over her thighs, cupped her breasts and cinched her waist. It made him think of red, pouty lips and a vermilion-satin-draped bed.

Her gaze met his and he was stunned at the in-tensity of her blue eyes, the color of cornflowers, the lashes thick and lush. Eyes that were usually covered with lenses from a pair of horn-rimmed glasses.

She wore gloss on her lips, accentuating the soft mouth, the pouting, kissable lips until he wanted to go to her and finally know what it was like to crush his mouth down onto hers.

He dreamed how that mouth would feel against his skin, around his aching cock, all over his body.

"Mr. St. James?" the judge said impatiently.

Jericho snapped out of his trance and said, "I have no more questions for this witness, Your Honor."

He walked back to the prosecutor's table and had to school his features. He sat down and closed his eyes as her warm breath flowed over his ear, sending heat arrowing into his groin.

He had no business getting a hard-on for a co-worker. It was deadly stupid, and it had to stop.

"I'm so sorry that I was late."

He nodded once without turning around, directing his attention to what the defense attorney was asking of his witness in case he had to object. But another part of his brain still reeled over the transformation of the woman he'd worked with for three years.

It wasn't the co-worker he was used to, but the woman who had played a nightly role in his sexual fantasies come to life. In his mind, he'd taken her every way a man could.

The defense attorney asked a leading question and Jericho objected neatly, receiving a sustain from the judge.

The defense attorney finished his questioning and the judge excused the witness.

Jericho stood and said, "The State calls Katherine Quinn to the stand."

She stood. The displacement of air as she rose

wafted over him. A subtle scent hit his nostrils, unfolding inside him like a seductive tease. Jericho turned his head just as she moved through the wooden gate railing that separated the courtroom from the gallery. She passed between the defense and the prosecution tables and it was as if time slowed.

He sensed every male eye in the room was on her as she glided across the polished wood floor, the sling backs making a soft clicking sound. The slow swing of her arms covered demurely in red knit, the crisscross of the material across her breasts, leaving her neck bare where a ruby glowed blood-red against her golden skin.

With a shock he realized that Kate's hair reached past her shapely butt. It was gorgeous multihues of blond and gold. Slowly she raised her hand and repeated the oath. With a rustle of cloth against her legs, she sat down.

Jericho pulled his professionalism around him like a cloak and stood, buttoning the jacket of his double-breasted, blue pin-striped suit.

He approached the witness stand and said, ''Hello, Ms. Quinn.''

She smiled brilliantly, showing perfect white teeth.

''Could you state your name for the record?''

"Katherine Quinn." Her husky voice caressed his ears.

"Where are you employed?" Focus on the questions, he told himself fiercely, not on her delectable mouth.

"The crime lab for the City of San Diego," she replied, and licked her lips as if she'd heard his thoughts.

"What is your job title, and what are your duties?"

"I'm a Criminalist III. My duties include examining, testing and analyzing tissue samples, chemical substances, physical materials and ballistics evidence. I interpret laboratory findings and tests along with collecting and preserving criminal evidence. I confer with ballistics, fingerprinting, handwriting, electronics, medical, chemical or metallurgical experts. I reconstruct crime scenes, prepare reports or presentations and provide expert witness testimony on evidence or laboratory techniques in trials or hearings."

"What education do you have that qualifies you to perform these duties?" He put his hand on the edge of the witness stand and came within a hairbreadth of hers. The heat from her skin reached out to his and he instantly pulled his hand away, resolving to keep his cool.

When she started, her voice was breathless, but it

firmed as she spoke. "I hold a Bachelor of Science in Biochemistry and Chemistry from the University of California at San Diego and a Masters of Forensic Science from George Washington University. I also continue to participate in on-going training."

"Approximately how many times have you testified regarding DNA profiling in court?"

"Hundreds."

"Can you explain to the court what DNA is?"

"DNA, or the scientific term deoxyribonucleic acid, is a very long, complex molecule that is located in the nucleus of each cell in the human body."

She continued and he had to admire the way she expertly described a complicated process for the easy comprehension of the jury.

As she continued, Jericho noted how she made eye contact with the jury and periodically him and the defense attorney.

"How does this scientific information result in DNA fingerprinting?" Jericho said, moving closer to the jury and making eye contact with each member. He was gratified to see that they were riveted to Kate's description and her testimony. It was imperative that she keep the explanations simple.

She smiled easily and launched into her response. "The chemical structure of everyone's DNA is the same. The only difference between people is the order of the base pairs. There are so many millions of base pairs in each person's DNA that every person has a different sequence.''

''And this allows you to perform DNA fingerprinting?'' Jericho prompted.

''No. These patterns do not, however, give an individual 'fingerprint,' but they are able to determine whether two DNA samples are from the same person, related people or nonrelated people. Scientists use a small number of sequences of DNA that are known to vary among individuals a great deal, and analyze those to get a certain probability of a match.''

''Are there tests available to detect an individual's genetic type?''

''Yes.''

''What test was used in the case?''

''Restriction fragment length polymorphism or R.F.L.P. Scientists can analyze the genetic patterns which appear in a person's DNA.''

''Is this test used in other fields?''

''Yes, in medical diagnostics, paternity testing or for the identification of missing persons.''

''Can you explain briefly how the test is conducted?'' When Kate finished with the brief explanation, he checked the jury again and was gratified to see they still hung on her every word.

"Are controls performed to ensure that a reliable and accurate result is obtained?"

"Yes."

"Can you describe the safeguards and controls used to ensure the integrity of the test?"

"Procedures are in place for careful collection of samples, a documented chain of custody, and strict guidelines for handling of DNA samples in the lab."

"Did you conduct a DNA test on the crime scene and reference samples in this case?"

"Yes."

"What were the results of the test?"

"In my opinion, the genetic profile of the crime scene blood sample and the known blood sample, identified as belonging to Duncan Carver, the defendant, are a match."

Jericho gave the jury time to absorb her words. This, after all, was the punch line. "What is the chance that this same genetic profile would be found in a random member of the population?"

"The probability is one out of twenty billion that Mr. Carver's DNA sample matches anyone else in the population."

"Are there samples that can be retested should someone wish to dispute the accuracy of the result?"

"Yes."

"Thank you, Ms. Quinn." Jericho turned toward

the judge. "I have no more questions for this witness." He walked back to his table.

Stan Marker, the defense attorney, didn't look pleased. The interested look of the jury and the extent of Kate's testimony damaged his case.

Kate watched as Stan stood and approached her. He smiled at her as if he was her best friend. Kate knew otherwise; she'd had experience with Stan before. The word smarmy came to mind along with the word letch.

"Based on the testimony you gave, it seems that you're sure the defendant is guilty. Would you like to see him convicted?"

Kate showed no reaction to Stan's question. She looked at Jericho and knew why he didn't object to the obvious leading question. He knew that Kate could handle it. "I have no opinion one way or the other. I am here to present the facts and will abide by the court's decision."

Stan didn't say anything for a moment. It was a defense attorney's trick called the silent treatment. He was hoping she would embellish her answer and give him ammunition to fire more leading questions.

When she didn't respond, but waited patiently for his next question, he changed tacks. "Your résumé seems to be lacking, Ms. Quinn, in that, you don't have a Ph.D."

"That is true, but I've worked in this field for six

years and have conducted and analyzed thousands of DNA samples.''

He frowned and leaned in, trying to either distract her or to intimidate her.

''Isn't it true that an advanced degree would enhance your abilities to do your job?''

Kate waited a beat, letting the irritation drain out of her. She wasn't going to let him rattle her. ''Most Ph.D.'s are theoretical and abstract. I don't see where it would enhance my job. Specialized hands-on courses in, say, Advanced DNA Methods or DNA-PCR STR Analysis and Typing are more beneficial.''

''I see.'' He moved away from the stand, formulating his next question. ''Isn't it possible that a sample collected in a careless or sloppy manner can create a potential for contamination?''

''Yes, it is possible. However, in my experience, given the many controls performed, such contamination would be detected.''

''I have no more questions for this witness,'' Stan said as he turned to the judge. He walked back to his table.

The judge turned toward Jericho. ''Mr. St. James, would you like to redirect?''

''No, Your Honor.''

''The witness may step down.''

Kate rose and was very careful not to look at Jericho, Stan or the defendant as she made her way back to her seat. To do so could indicate to the jury that she had a biased opinion.

"The State rests," Jericho said.

The judge nodded and addressed Stan. "We'll begin with the defense's case tomorrow morning at nine o'clock sharp." The judge banged his gavel. "Court is adjourned."

Everyone stood as the judge left. Kate walked toward the door to the outside hall. "Kate," Stan called as he came up to her. "You were like a rock on the stand. Couldn't move you."

"Just telling the truth."

He nodded, his eyes caressing her body, making her skin crawl. "Nice dress. I had no idea you were so beautiful. Say the word and I'll be your love slave," Stan said, but Kate was barely paying attention.

Out of the corner of her eye, Jericho collected his papers. He never even glanced her way. Her heart sank. He was just not interested in her. Not even with her new dress or her altered look. He shut his briefcase and walked toward them.

She was going to have to tell Sienna Parker and Lana Dempsey that she'd failed miserably. Over drinks, the three best friends had discussed the man Sienna had walked into the club with and Lana had dared Sienna to go after him after Sienna insinuated that Lana was afraid to go after her co-worker, Sean O'Neill. Then they'd turned on her. Both of them knowing that Kate had the hots for Jericho.

Kate was tired of the nickname ''Sister Kate'' and she'd grabbed at the dare with both hands.

She looked away in disappointment.

''Makes me want to get into your genes,'' Stan persisted, laughing at his pun.

Kate opened her mouth to tell the letch off but Jericho's deep, mesmerizing voice interrupted her.

''Watch your mouth, Stan, or I'll bring you up on charges for sexual harassment,'' Jericho threatened. He was suddenly looming over the little creep's shoulder.

Kate gasped at his sudden presence and Stan flushed.

''Sorry, Kate. Just trying to make a very lame joke.''

Jericho dismissed Stan and turned to her. ''Kate, could I see you in my office?''

''I should get back to the lab.'' The disappointment was too much to bear. She just couldn't sit across a desk from him and pretend as though his ambivalence didn't affect her.

''It'll only take a few moments.''

Stan took the opportunity to leave and Kate faced off with Jericho. Why did the full force of the man make her heart beat like a hummingbird trapped in her chest?

Taking a measured breath, Kate shoved her hair behind her shoulders. She wasn't into self-deception. Nor would she insult her own intelligence by writing off her scrutiny of the deputy district attorney to her scientist's honed observation skills. It hadn't been the scientist in her who'd noted that D.D.A. Jericho St. James's fine, aesthetic face, slash of cheekbones and sculpted mouth made him almost ridiculously handsome. And it hadn't been the scientist who'd jolted when his fiercely intelligent caramel eyes locked with hers, nor whose nerves faintly hummed when the glow from the overhead lights picked up warm threads of tawny highlights in brown hair as thick as melted chocolate.

"There wasn't any need to protect me, Mr. D.D.A. Stan's unarmed."

"Unarmed?"

"Yeah, can't cross wits with the witless."

"I don't care. It's time he learned that there's zero tolerance for the mistreatment of women."

That shut Kate's mouth. Rich brown eyes, riveting in their intensity, held her immobile.

Professionally, Kate knew all there was to know about Jericho. He'd graduated from Columbia Law School with honors, was one of the most successful prosecutors in San Diego's history, and was a tough and demanding taskmaster to her and her co-workers.

She followed him out of the courtroom and down the narrow hallway, passing numerous small offices. There was many a long day or night spent in those tight, enclosed spaces going over court testimony, discussing a multitude of other issues with one D.D.A. or another.

"Would you like some coffee?" Jericho asked as they rounded a corner. When he stepped beside her, she caught a hint of his masculine scent.

For an instant, she couldn't concentrate on anything but the powerful effect of him, the lust that traveled through her system so that she had to close her eyes to keep her composure.

She was too aware, she told herself while she struggled against the hot sensations that curled around her whenever she was in this man's presence.

"No. No coffee, thank you." Frowning, she fought the rush of irritation at the easy way he had of dismissing her sexuality. It wasn't fair that he wasn't as affected by her presence as she was by his.

Behind a very neat desk, a young, pert receptionist sat behind a shoulder-high counter flanked by file cabinets, telephone switchboard and computer.

"Hold my calls, Sandy," Jericho said.

Jericho pushed open the door and said, "After you."

Kate walked in and looked around at a familiar sight. Disorderly piles of folders sat on a credenza against the back wall and were stacked on the end of his desk, leaving most of the massive wooden desk clear.

How, she wondered, could Jericho St. James be so tough in court, so scrupulous in his appearance, yet work in such a cluttered office?

She glanced over at him as he closed the office door. What lay beneath that cool, controlled prosecutor's image? Fire?

He leaned against the door and folded his arms. "Have a seat."

Kate ignored the words and set her purse down onto one of the chairs. His scrutiny made her nervous. Was he trying to figure out why she'd changed her appearance, or had he even noticed.

She walked around the room, looking at his plaques and framed certificates hanging on the gray walls. Besides his diplomas there were other honors that lauded his service and documented his membership in professional organizations. She noted the stark absence of photos of loved ones, no pictures of vacations, no sports trophies, no plants. His office gave her no idea of the inner workings of Jericho the man. He pushed off the door and walked to his desk, sitting casually on the edge, his intense gaze following her every move. Still, she knew all she wanted to know about him. She wanted him in her bed. She wanted to wrap herself around him, to kiss the provocative curve of his mouth. It irked her that she'd planned every aspect of her grand entrance and he hadn't had one reaction to her new look.

"What did you want to talk to me about?"

"Your testimony was flawless."

Kate turned toward him and narrowed her eyes. "Is that why you brought me here?"

"No. I wanted to let you know that your testimony won my case. But it could have gone differently if you hadn't arrived on time. I would have had to explain it to the judge and the jury would have wondered if I was stalling. I have to be able to depend on you, Kate."

"I'm sorry. I almost missed the bus." Kate sat in one of the chairs while Jericho went behind his desk.

Jericho's lips curved, but the smile wasn't reflected in his eyes. "The bus?"

"I couldn't get a cab," she replied coolly.

Jericho shrugged out of his suit coat. "Don't you have a car?"

Kate felt her breath go shallow while she measured the broad span of shoulders beneath his starched white shirt. Her eyes flicked downward. His waist was compact, his hips lean. The body, she decided, was as impressive as the face.

"Yes, I have a car."

"Am I missing something here?"

"My car wouldn't start this morning and I had to run for the bus."

"That must have been some sight."

For the first time since she'd met Jericho St. James she saw him look uncomfortable. "I shouldn't have made that comment."

"No. Tell me. I want to know what you mean."

He was looking at her, trapping her in a masculine force field of crackling heat. He frightened her in his intensity, his eyes so hot and hungry. "You have great legs, Kate," he said. "That dress…"

Because she had never seen Jericho like this, she stared at him, openmouthed, extremely aware of the way her nipples rasped against the fabric of her bra, the slide of the knit against her skin as breath heaved in her lungs. Her face was hot, her lips felt sensitive. Small tremors racked her body. The look in his eyes pulled at something deep inside her; a verdant, hidden place that budded and bloomed under his gaze, aching with nameless longing.

The door banged open and the D.A. bustled in. "Jericho…." he trailed off. "Sorry. Didn't know you had someone in your office. How are you, Kate?"

D.A. Matt Roth sat in the other chair and Kate abruptly stood, unable to even process the D.A.'s question in regard to her health. Right now, she needed to get out before she punched Jericho out.

''There's no need for you to leave,'' the D.A. said good-naturedly. ''I'll only be a moment.''

''That's okay, sir. We were finished.''

''Not quite, Kate,'' Jericho said, shades of meaning coloring his words.

''We're not?''

''Next time you need to testify for me, do me a favor and be on time.''

She nodded and backed out of the room, closing the door behind her.

She waited until she was a good distance away from his office before she swore vehemently under her breath. Heat infused her and it had nothing to do with Jericho's sexy mouth or husky voice. It was a hot, blue-flame-special, steam-from-the-ears anger. How *dare* he pretend all this time to be unmoved by her? *How dare he?*

She burst out of the courthouse into the street, scanning the sidewalk for cabs as she marched to the curb. She faintly heard the D.A. call her name as he hurried up to her.

She'd show Jericho St. James. The resolve burned in her like fire. He would be hers. She would make sure of it.

She would tease him, entice him, and in the end when he was hers, she would make him beg.

2

JERICHO SAT IMMOBILE behind his desk after the D.A. left. He'd blundered, and blundered big. She couldn't mistake his interest. It had been building in him for weeks. The fantasies of her had become more powerful until he was doing it during the day instead of dreaming about her at night.

She was seductive danger. He saw the potential in her. It was there like a whisper of sensation across his skin. He could see it in the curve of her cheekbone, the cool line of her neck. It wasn't that Kate wasn't experienced. He sensed she was. It was more that she hadn't been awakened.

But therein lay Jericho's dilemma. He could unlock the secrets of her body. He could feel it every time she came near him—through the starched lab coat and the dark-rimmed glasses and the flat-heeled shoes.

He sensed that Kate could be his body and soul.

It made him shake sometimes to know how much she wanted him. He could see it in her eyes.

But more dangerous by far was how much he wanted her.

She was unaware of how deep her sexuality affected him until only a few moments ago when he'd let only a fraction of it show. It had seeped out, unable to be contained because Kate in that red dress made him forget the danger and only concentrate on the sweetness.

She was still unaware that he'd go down on his knees for one taste of her. But like a drug, one taste wouldn't satisfy him. He knew his limit and he sensed with Kate that there wouldn't be one. Better not to take that first sip.

But the dangers were still there, still viable.

Professional danger: In that he worked with her; it just wouldn't be smart to mix business and pleasure.

Emotional danger: When he thought about her eyes, soft and tender for him, his chest tightened. It caused a vortex of need. And in its center stood Katherine Quinn.

The hard part? Resisting the irresistible, delectable, unawakened Kate Quinn.

The easy part? Hell, there wasn't any easy part.

The impossible? Not losing himself in her if he was weak enough or stupid enough to even think about touching her.

KATE TOOK HER STAIRS two at a time. She was already going to be an hour late to the D.A.'s announcement party. Tonight the D.A. would name the person whom he'll back in the upcoming elections. Support from D.A. Matt Roth was a strong endorsement indeed. When he caught up to her after she'd left Jericho's office, he'd invited her as she'd fumed at the curb.

She almost ran into Danny Hamilton at the top of the stairs to her third-floor apartment.

"Whoa, there, Miss Kate. You could fall and hurt yourself real bad." His hands steadied her.

Danny Hamilton smiled at her and Kate couldn't help but smile back at his infectious grin.

Danny was twenty-five and the maintenance man for the building. He was as sweet as they came and mildly retarded.

"I fixed the leak in your bathroom. Weren't nothing but a faulty washer. Now, I'm holding you to those chocolate-chip cookies you promised."

Kate smiled. "Sunday soon enough?"

"Aw, how about tonight?"

He looked so crestfallen, Kate said, "I would Danny, but I can't. I've been invited to a party and I'm spending Saturday with friends."

He nodded. "That's good, Miss Kate. You don't get out enough, a pretty lady like you."

"I'm running a little late, so I'll see you on Sunday. I'll save you the comics."

He smiled and whistled as he went down the stairs. She slammed into her apartment already untying the red wrap dress. The phone rang as she peeled the clingy knit away from her arms.

"Hello?"

"Hi, Kate. I have Lana on, too," Sienna said.

"He didn't try to hide it," Kate said, the anger starting to build in her again.

"If he wasn't moved by that kicking dress, I'd say he has to be gay," Lana blurted.

She smiled as her friend jumped to her defense. "Simmer down, Lana. He's been hiding it all this time."

"What do you mean?" Sienna asked.

"I saw the heat in his eyes and, oh, baby, was it hot."

"That jerk," Lana said.

"What are you going to do?" Sienna asked.

"Make him crazy for it," Kate said with relish.

"Way to go, Sister Kate. Kick that nun's habit to the curb," Lana said.

"Oh, Jericho will be praying, all right. He'll be praying for mercy when I get done with him."

Both of her friends broke out in laughter, but Kate didn't crack a smile. She was dead serious.

ONE HOUR INTO the announcement dinner, the ballroom was packed. From her vantage point at the top of the stairs, she caught eddies of color and bits of conversation from the elegantly dressed guests standing beneath the spill of light from crystal-rich chandeliers. Waiters carrying trays loaded with champagne flutes eased their way through the crowd. The air was permeated with designer perfume, punctuated here and there with laughter. Over the humming din she could hear the soft strains of a piano and sax.

She made her way down the staircase. The Grand Ballroom of the Wilmore Hotel was awash with brightness, reflecting the soft pink roses that wound around the two massive columns framing the entrance. And the bottom of each column was encircled with blood-red roses. It was a stunning contrast.

It took her only a moment to identify the man standing next to one of those columns. Her temper spiked. Her breath got trapped in her lungs. He was incredibly handsome and her heart kicked into a fluttering pace when he moved toward her. In a suit, he was irresistibly male. In a tuxedo, Jericho St. James held a magnetic quality that squeezed her heart until she thought it'd burst.

The austere contrast of the snowy-white shirt against the black tux should have made him look civilized and conventional. Instead it contrasted with his dangerous good looks, highlighting them. His dark hair curved around the satiny collar and made her knees go weak.

His eyes were purposeful, his look, intense. And it made her feel as if she were the only woman in the world.

His eyes traveled over her in a slow slide that made Kate's knees weak. She'd purposely chosen the black dress for its dramatic baring of her midriff beneath see-through black mesh. The same material made up the whole back of the dress that plunged to her waist. A tight black skirt with sheer black thigh-highs finished off the effect.

As her black satin sandal hit the marble floor, Jericho came up to her. Kate smiled, remembering Lana's instruction on enticing him to touch her in innocent ways. She'd practiced unclasping the diamond necklace around her neck and she did so now. With a soft cry, she tried to catch it as it fell.

But Jericho's big hand easily caught it.

When she reached to take it from him, he said, ''Let me.'' He moved behind her and gently grasped the delicate chain. She couldn't control the quick intake of breath when his warm hands touched the nape of her neck. He expertly clasped the necklace, sending goose bumps along her skin.

His hands lingered, but Kate pretended not to notice. She wanted nothing more than to lean into those elegant hands, the heated sensation intoxicating.

But she stepped away from him and turned.

"I had no idea you'd be here," he said.

"The D.A. invited me after I left your office." She shifted her gaze to the milling crowd.

"You're late. Did you miss the bus?"

His teasing tone caught her off guard as she pulled her gaze from the couples locked in sensual embraces. His eyes danced. This wasn't going to be easy. She almost wished for the cool, distant Jericho. Resisting this smiling, teasing Jericho would take all her willpower. "No. I took a cab this time. I was late leaving the office."

"The conscientious Ms. Quinn," he said, leaning in, his warm breath caressing her ear, making her insides clench.

She turned toward him, her eyes narrowing. "What is that supposed to mean?"

"Just that you used to be predictable," he groused.

"That sounds boring."

"No, I'd call it safe. I could always count on that lab coat and those glasses. What happened?"

"I don't want to play it safe anymore."

"Being reckless holds tough consequences." His voice was soft, but it sent chills through her entire body.

"Jericho, *sweetheart,* found you at last!"

Taken aback by the woman's exuberance, Kate stepped away to avoid being knocked over by the woman hurrying up to them. Two men followed in her wake, one with gray hair, and the other, a younger version. She was somewhere in her late twenties with red hair that could only have come out of a bottle and was cut as short as a boy's. Her curvy body accentuated by golden sequins was impressive. The be-ringed hand she'd closed over Jericho's arm revealed long nails with blood-red polish.

She kissed Jericho full on the mouth then scolded, "You're a *bad boy* to try to elude me. Tell me you know who's going to be named as Roth's successor."

"I've been sworn to secrecy," Jericho stated.

Making a moue of displeasure, the woman slid her arm through Jericho's, then turned her attention to Kate.

"Well, if you won't tell me, you difficult man, then you must introduce me to your lovely companion."

"Of course," Jericho said smoothly. "Katherine Quinn, meet Samantha Caldwell, the new crime beat reporter for the *San Diego Times.*"

"Call me Kate." She took the hand Samantha offered.

Samantha turned to the two men. "This is George Mitchell and his son Ken."

"Mitchell? That's the name of my apartment building," Kate said.

"Mitchell Downtown Apartments?" Ken said smoothly.

"Yes."

"My father owns that building." Ken Mitchell fit the image of the all-American boy. A tuxedo encased his tall, athletic body to perfection; the overhead lights turned his jet-black hair to gleaming ebony. But there was something about him that made her instincts instantly sit up and take notice.

"What do you do, Ms. Quinn?" Samantha asked.

Kate focused on the reporter. "I'm a criminalist."

"Oo-ooh, a CSI type. How wonderful." She leaned in, whispering like a co-conspirator. "I suppose you wouldn't know who he's going to support."

"No, I'm sorry. He hasn't confided in me."

Samantha studied them. "You two seem so cozy. Work closely together, do you?"

The insinuation in her voice was clear.

Kate's spine went stiff. "Just a minute…" Kate said in protest.

But Samantha talked right over her. "Now, I must have a dance." She turned to Kate and smiled.

"Don't worry, dear," Samantha soothed. "I don't have designs on him."

Samantha dragged Jericho out onto the dance floor and Kate watched for a short time. Needing sustenance, she grabbed a flute of champagne from one of the trays carried by the mingling waiters.

"Don't worry about Sam. She really doesn't have designs on your prosecutor. She has designs on me," Ken Mitchell said with a self-satisfied smirk on his face.

Taking a sip, she watched Jericho move smoothly and effortlessly with the gregarious reporter. Who did the woman think she was kidding? If Samantha didn't want Jericho for herself, Kate would eat her shoe. Ken Mitchell wasn't blind or stupid, so that left arrogant.

"Are you trying to convince me or yourself?" Kate said in an uncharacteristic outburst, wiping the smile off his face.

Discarding the champagne flute, she marched out onto the dance floor. She tapped Samantha on the shoulder and said, "I'm sure you won't mind if I cut in, *dear*. I'm sure Ken is getting lonely."

Samantha stepped back and Kate slid right into Jericho's arms.

"Nothing I love to see more than a person put in her place," he said, looking down into her face. "I always knew you had a backbone of steel, Kate."

"My mother would call it a formidable will."

"Your mother's an astute woman."

"Yes, she is."

"Is she in law enforcement, too?"

"No. She cleans houses for people like you."

"People like me?"

"Rich."

"That sounded almost accusatory. How do you know that I'm one of *those* people?"

"I can tell from your expensive taste in Armani suits and Gucci shoes. No prosecutor can afford such items on his salary."

"Your keen scientist's eye. No wonder you're so good at crime scene investigation."

"So why did you choose prosecution over your daddy's law firm?"

"You're so sure of yourself?"

She raised her eyebrows. "Tell me I'm wrong."

"It wasn't my father's law firm, but you're close. An uncle."

"Hmm. So why a prosecutor?"

"I want to put away bad guys where they can't hurt anyone else. Get to the truth of the crime and see justice served."

His answer surprised her. She had always thought of Jericho as a competitor with a killer body and gorgeous face. Sure she knew he was a proficient prosecutor, but to hear his motivation for his intensity in court rocked her.

"I thought you just liked to win."

"I do like to win, but I want the truth, too."

They fell silent and Kate rested her face against Jericho's neck, taking in the scent of him. As he turned, she could see through the dancing couples that Ken and George Mitchell were arguing. It looked like quite a heated battle. Ken's face was flushed red, his eyes were narrowed and flashing. She watched as he snarled at his father then stalked away.

There was something very tense between Ken and his father. Something that made him very angry.

When the music ended, Jericho maneuvered Kate through the French doors that opened onto a balcony. He turned and shut them against the light and low hum of conversation from the ballroom.

"I think I'd like another dance," Kate said, feeling all of a sudden boxed in by Jericho's presence and the closed French doors.

She went past him, but she found herself stopped, pinned by his big body, the heat of his breath on the back of her neck. "Do you think I didn't notice you in your red dress, Kate?"

The dark current in his voice threatened to pull her under, into heated, unknown depths. She writhed in his tight grasp and the fluttering surge of desire caught her tight in a hot fist. "You've never noticed me at all, Jericho. Why do you think I wore the red dress?"

"You mean, you changed your look for me?" Damn, what a turn-on. "But what you don't know is that I've fantasized about you from the moment I met you. You are sleeping, Kate, and I want to be the one to awaken you."

Kate tried to speak, but her lungs heaved from the shock of his admission and his weight as he pressed her tighter to the wall.

"I thought it prudent to refrain from getting involved with a co-worker," Jericho said, "But it hasn't been easy to keep my hands off you."

A spurt of anger made her reckless. Kate found her voice and said softly, "Who said anything about involvement? I want hot, raw, out-of-control sex."

Jericho jerked away from her body. The silence between them stretched out. She wasn't going to move or speak. She was going to torture him. Watch him twist in the flames with that knowing look in her eyes.

Kate shivered at the way his eyes searched hers as if he could see right through her. All the way down to the sweet, restless ache that pulsed inside her, where the wild woman waited, naked and willing and wanton. The knowledge of her deepest, hidden secret was bare in his eyes. He knew perfectly well how much she wanted him. He'd always known.

But it was only dawning on her now, this minute, how much he wanted her.

That turned *her* on. She tried to remember that this was supposed to be about teasing and begging, but she got lost in the swirl of his sinfully dark eyes.

Jericho gathered the mass of her hair into his hand and buried his face against the rippling strands.

She let out a startled cry as he seized her, hauling her up against the hard contours of his body.

His arms tightened around her and he stared into her eyes. As fierce and intent as if he could read her mind.

His heat scorched her. His muscles firm and hot, burning her through the thin fabric of her dress. His breath was as rapid as her own.

Jericho made a harsh sound deep in his throat and his arms tightened around her with steely strength. It was as if he could read her purpose to only tease him relentlessly, to make him get down on his knees and beg her.

With a mocking slant to his mouth, he fused his lips to hers, a searing, devouring kiss unlike anything she had ever known or imagined. She was dragged into it headlong, intoxicated by his voracious energy, the taste of him almost familiar, yet not. He smelled so good—soap and starch, and a unique smell of his own, warm and enticing, like cinnamon. His jaw was rough; his sensual mouth coaxed hers open. Eager, bold and delicious.

She wanted to writhe against him, to crawl inside his skin, to touch everything, to taste everything. He was so strong, bursting with fierce energy, and she ached with hunger for it. His thick shaft pressed against her, rock-hard, radiating heat.

It was the press of his flesh to hers that brought her shockingly to her own senses. No. This was too easy. She was committed, and hurtling forward into the unknown, but it would be on her terms.

She pulled away from him and stepped back. She opened her mouth, praying that something coherent would come out. "What do you want, Jericho?"

"You."

"Good. I've wanted you for months, but you already knew that."

A muscle pulsed in his jaw and his eyes narrowed. A prickle of unease mixed into the shimmering, giddy alchemy of her excitement.

Danger.

She wanted to stroke the fine, elegant planes of his face, to soothe the pulsations of need and desire that emanated from him. The scarlet of desire and gold of pleasure flashed across her in dazzling promise like dream images.

"Kate…"

She turned and walked away from him. It was the hardest thing she'd ever done, but she was determined to let him know that she wasn't a pushover, that he couldn't play her like a witness on the stand. This time she was going to call the shots.

She turned and gave him a coy look. "It's your turn to wait."

3

KATE WAS SMILING as she hailed a cab. Getting into the vehicle when it stopped, she settled onto the back seat.

The look on his face had been priceless.

Kate pulled out her cell phone and dialed Lana, who answered on the first ring.

"I had him eating out of my hand," Kate said.

Lana laughed. "Looks like we're going to have to find a new nickname for you. You sound like you're thoroughly enjoying Mr. St. James's discomfort."

"Serves him right."

"For pretending he doesn't want you?" Lana asked.

"Yes. Punitive damages for mental and sexual cruelty."

"Sexual cruelty?" Lana said with a smile in her voice.

Kate giggled. "Okay, so that's a stretch. I did everything but swing from the chandelier to get his attention."

"I feel your pain and I think you should make him work for it. Sounds like Jericho usually gets what he wants."

A thrill went down Kate's spine. The thought of all that male intensity trained on her made her both nervous and wet.

Kate's phone beeped. "Lana, I've got another call. I'll talk to you tomorrow."

"Make sure you call Sienna before you go to bed. She'll want to hear it from the horse's mouth."

"I will."

Kate disconnected and said, "Hello?"

She listened intently to the watch commander directing her to a crime scene. When he gave the address, Kate gasped. "Could you repeat that?" she asked. "Thanks, got it."

She disconnected the call and sat deeper into the seat. There was no need to give the cabbie any other direction. The murder scene was in her building.

THE CAB PULLED UP to her apartment complex and Kate stepped out. There were police cars parked in front, sirens casting a bluish-red glow over the cut stone of the building.

A policeman stopped her. "Residents and police personnel only, ma'am."

"I'm both, McMasters."

The officer looked at her and then recognition

dawned across his face. His eyes traveled over the bodice of her dress, lingered on her midriff showing through the sheer black cloth and then gaped at her.

"Do you think I could get to the crime scene?" Kate said, rolling her eyes.

"Kate, is that you?"

"Yes, it's me."

"Wow! You look amazing."

"Thanks, McMasters," she said, laughing as she glided past him, beginning to like her new persona.

Kate entered the apartment building and faced another officer who also gave her the once-over. If this kept up, she was going to get a big head.

Finally she was directed to the first-floor apartment and the homicide detective handling the case.

Sienna Parker, flanked by Tom Sanders, a tall, competent veteran, greeted her at the door. She saw the male appreciation in his eyes, but he was more professional than the beat cops had been.

"Hi, Sienna. What are you doing here?"

"Kate, good to see you," Tom answered. "She's on loan from burglary. We're short staffed."

"So what do we have?"

"The vic's daughter came over for dinner and found the apartment unlocked and her mother in the bathroom." Sienna looked down at her notepad. "A Mrs. Marie LePlante." She walked into the hall as she talked. "She has an abrasion on her temple, but no other marks on the body."

"How much blood?"

"Not much at all."

There was a flurry of noise and her partner stuck his head in the doorway. "Kinda fancy for a crime scene, Kate," Eric Banner said, looking her up and down.

"Yeah, yeah, I've been hearing it all night. I was at a party." She waved him off, knowing Eric would keep up the teasing for some time. He was tall, dark and handsome. She was asked by many of her female co-workers if there was anything between them. But Kate wasn't interested in Eric that way. They were just good friends and had an excellent working relationship. "Has the M.E. been here yet?"

"Been and gone. Said she's only been dead half hour to an hour. I really like the new look," he said with a smirk.

"Thanks. I'll take the bathroom and the vic, Eric."

He reached out and handed her her kit. "Sure. I'll take the rest of the apartment."

"I've already had a good look at the vic. I'm going to start talking to the neighbors. You'll get me your notes when you're finished?" Sienna asked.

"Yes, but it may take a couple of days."

"No problem," Sienna said, and left.

Tom went to walk out the door, but stopped. "I like the new look, too, Kate. Very classy. Don't listen to Banner."

Kate smiled at the man old enough to be her father. "Thanks, Sanders."

He smiled and slipped out the door.

Kate took her time examining the bathroom, noted where the shower doors were, the towels that were lying on the floor and the disarray of the sink. Shards from a broken full-length mirror next to the sink lay on the floor. On closer examination, Kate saw blood on several pieces of glass. The vic had struggled with her attacker. Kate made copious notes on a wire-bound notebook she'd removed from her case. She took her camera from the bag and photographed the whole bathroom, including the broken mirror and the tiny dropletss of blood on the sink.

She opened her kit, and reached for a set of rubber gloves and pulled them on. Grabbing the chalk, she ran a quick line around the body. She examined the fingernails and took scrapings. She paused in her examination of the body for other forensic evidence; she'd have to make sure that she got the clothes bagged and returned to her.

The flap of the robe covered the woman's neck. Curious, Kate took a pen and pushed the flap back. Faintly, she could see marks just forming on the woman's neck. Looked as though she'd been strangled, but Kate never jumped to conclusions until the M.E. gave his report.

She picked up each bloody shard from the floor with tweezers and set them in a row to dry. She gathered samples of blood off the sink.

Next, she moved to the shower and took a moment to look around inside. Squatting, she noticed dirt and hair fibers. Using her tweezers, she collected the hair, making a mental note to vacuum in here before she left.

Rising to her full height, Kate rubbed at her neck and rolled her shoulders. She looked at her watch and saw that it had already been three hours since she'd walked into the crime scene. She lifted one foot out of her classy black sandal, then the other. They did great things for her legs and were very sexy, but right now she wished for her comfortable flat-heeled shoes.

She went back to her kit, pulled out her measuring tape and started the tedious job of measuring and sketching every part of the room.

"Hey, you done yet?" The EMT put his head into the room, careful not to walk into the area.

"Yes, you can take the body."

After securing her kit and her evidence, she walked out of the bathroom to give the two EMTs enough room to maneuver. Eric was in the living room gathering fibers from the rug.

"I need to vacuum the shower."

"It's on the kitchen table."

Kate walked into the kitchen and picked up the vacuum and did what she had to do in the bathroom.

She went back out to the living room just as Ken Mitchell came through the front door.

"What are you doing here?" Kate asked.

"I wanted to know when this apartment would be cleared so that it can be cleaned and rented again. Time is money." His voice was cool and smooth as if he'd just asked about the weather.

She was surprised to see that he had changed. She knew it was only eleven o'clock and was sure the party would have gone on longer.

His dark linen slacks and loose-fitting white shirt lent him an elegant look, as if he'd just come from a casual gathering at the country club.

He walked deeper into the room and Kate held up her hand. "No further. This is a crime scene."

Something flashed in his eyes, his mouth pulling into a hard line. Kate had the sense that the glossy veneer of sophistication and charm was a thin coat over a troubled, unstable surface.

Eric slid her a glance and she raised her brows. "The crime scene will be sealed for at least three days."

"By whose authority?" he countered.

"Mine."

"In three days?" He glanced at Eric, then back at her.

"See me again and I'll let you know if it'll be longer." She handed him her business card, careful not to let her skin touch his.

Mitchell nodded, accepting the card. He turned to leave.

"Did you know Mrs. LePlante?" Kate asked.

His gaze probed her face, then lowered and inched down her body. Kate's skin crawled. "Who?"

"The tenant in this apartment. The one who was killed tonight."

"No. I…uh…didn't," he murmured.

Ken opened the apartment door.

"You done here, Eric?" Kate asked.

"Just about."

"Could you give me a lift back to the office?"

"Hey, I didn't do nothing! Let me go!"

The shouting from the hall interrupted them and Kate froze as she recognized the voice.

She hurried past Mitchell and saw Tom with his arm across Danny Hamilton's back. Sienna was close by.

"Tom, what's going on?" She saw the cuffs in

his hands and cried, ''Are you arresting Danny for this crime?''

''No. We just wanted him to come down to the station and have a talk. He got agitated.''

''Miss Kate. Help me,'' Danny pleaded.

''It's all right, Danny. Detective Sanders and his partner just want to ask you a few questions.''

''Will you be there?''

His little-boy-lost look nipped at her heart. ''Sure. I'll be there.''

''Do I get to ride in a police car?'' he asked.

Kate bit her lip to keep her emotions in check. ''Yes, you get to ride in a police car.''

''I'll go then.''

Tom nodded his thanks and took Danny out of the building. Sienna squeezed her arm before she followed them.

Eric came into the hall carrying his kit, evidence and vacuum. ''Were you just asking me for a ride?''

''Yes, my car is in the shop.''

''Sure.''

She turned to find Mitchell in her path.

''I'm sorry that I ever hired that dummy. If I hadn't, Mrs. LePlante might still be alive.'' He followed Danny's retreating back but when she expected to see disgust in his eyes, it looked suspiciously like guilt.

''There isn't any evidence that Danny had anything to do with Mrs. LePlante's death. Watch your mouth.''

She felt Eric's hand on her shoulder. She took a deep breath to regain her composure.

''Yeah, maybe not, but it doesn't excuse him for stealing.''

''What do you mean?'' Kate demanded.

''There's been a rash of burglaries in this building and Danny has the key to every apartment. According to the police, there wasn't any forced entry.''

''This is the first time I've heard anything about any burglaries,'' Kate said, her forehead creasing. She was beginning to dislike this man even more.

''We tried to keep it quiet and we're cooperating with the police.''

''If they had anything on Danny, they would have arrested him.''

Mitchell shrugged. ''Just a matter of time. Look, I'm sorry I stepped on your toes in there.''

Too polite, too remorseful, too…glossy. Instinct told Kate there was a volcano brewing beneath that smooth facade.

In silence, she watched his hand as he raised it, holding it out to her. His fingers were long, strong and tanned. Powerful. She wondered if he'd made the marks on Mrs. LePlante's neck.

She said nothing as he dropped his hand, brushed past Kate and left the building.

"What was that all about?" Eric asked.

"I don't know, but I don't like him," Kate said, watching Mitchell's retreating back.

She followed Eric out of her apartment building, set the kit and evidence on his back seat and got into the car.

"Word is that you danced with St. James tonight."

"Word travels fast."

"You know cops. We're the biggest gossipmongers around. Now fess up. Did you dance with him?"

"I danced with him. What of it?"

"Just askin', but now I'm curious as to why you have that defensive note in your voice. Is there something you want to tell your partner?"

"Like what, Banner. Maybe, you're a pain in my butt?"

He chuckled. "You already know that, Quinn. Like you changed your look overnight. Show up for work in that red dress. Wow, then tonight. That black dress is some concoction."

"So I did a makeover. No big deal."

"It is a big deal. St. James is one intense guy. I've seen him in court go for the jugular and then calmly clean off his claws like a big jungle cat."

"Are you saying that if I wanted to go after St. James, I may not be able to handle him?"

"I just don't want you to get hurt."

She looked at him and his face was earnest in the semidarkness. All trace of teasing and humor aside.

She reached out and squeezed his forearm. "Thanks for that brotherly advice, but I'm not afraid of St. James."

"I sure hope you know where to pet him to make him purr instead of growl."

"Either way. I can handle him."

Eric chuckled. "When you say it in that tone of voice, I believe it," he said as he pulled up to the police lab and let Kate off with the evidence. Eric would bring the kits and they'd restock them with the items they'd used tonight.

She went into the lab, properly cataloged and stored all the evidence, so that she could begin analyzing all the data later.

She made her way through the lab area and up into the police department. She stopped at the detectives' area and found out that Danny Hamilton was in Interrogation Three.

When Kate walked into the observation area, Jericho was already there, still in his tuxedo.

She zeroed in on his mouth, that mouth that only hours ago had shown her the gateway to heaven. She wanted nothing more than to feel that sculpted mouth pressed to hers.

He stared at her, his eyes sizzling brown coals.

Her breathing increased, her mouth tingled. His eyelids drooped, his hooded gaze dropping to her lips and the tingling turned into an ache. She licked her dry lips and heat flashed in his eyes.

"Kate," Captain Davis said, nodding to her. "Looks like we pulled you out of a party, too."

"Jericho—Mr. St. James and I were at the same function for D.A. Roth."

"Oh, so you know that Mr. St. James is the one running for the position backed by D.A. Roth."

Kate's gaze went to Jericho. "You're running for D.A.?"

"Yes. It was announced after you left."

"I see."

"Danny, we just want to know if you had a beef with Mrs. LePlante," Tom Sanders said from behind the one-way glass.

"She was a mean lady. She was always hitting me," Danny said sullenly.

"Did you hit her?" Sienna asked gently.

Kate moved to the one-way glass and her heart tightened in her chest to see the scared look on Danny's face.

Danny shook his head, but wouldn't look at Tom or Sienna. "I didn't like her."

"But did you hurt her?"

"Shouldn't he have a lawyer?" Kate blurted.

"Whose side are you on, Ms. Quinn? I thought you worked for us," Captain Davis said.

"Danny's a little slow."

"He's not under arrest right now, so technically he doesn't need a lawyer."

A uniformed cop came into the observation room. He whispered something in the captain's ear. The captain nodded and turned to Jericho.

"The search of Danny Hamilton's apartment has turned up a bloody brass candlestick."

"Who gave you permission to search?" Jericho asked.

The cop thumbed toward the glass. "The kid. Said we could go through anything we wanted."

"Why did you search his apartment?" Kate asked.

"Eyewitness stated that she heard Danny and Mrs. LePlante arguing. Then after that, she heard nothing. We went to the kid's apartment and he said we could search. Afterward he got really agitated when we wanted to bring him down to division to question him," the uniform said.

Jericho stood there quietly. "Arrest him."

"Charges?" Captain Davis asked.

"Second degree murder."

"But we don't even know what killed LePlante yet," Kate said.

"The evidence sounds concrete enough to go to the grand jury. Arrest him."

"Danny didn't do it. I know he couldn't have. He's not capable of hurting anyone," Kate persisted.

"Sounds like the evidence is proving you wrong," Captain Davis said, exiting the room and entering the interrogation room. He talked to Tom who got up and snapped cuffs on a bewildered and frightened Danny.

They exited the observation room just as Tom was leading Danny out of the interrogation room.

"Help me, Miss Kate. Don't let them lock me up. I didn't do nothing."

"Don't worry, Danny. It'll be okay. Go with the officers. I'll come and visit you as soon as I can."

"I'm scared, Miss Kate."

"I know, Danny. But it'll be all right. Don't worry."

She rounded on Jericho. "This is all a mistake."

"I'm sorry about this, Kate. But the evidence doesn't lie."

"I know, but I don't believe it. I know this man."

Kate walked with Jericho to the stairs where Eric was waiting. "Eric, what are you doing here?"

"You said your car was in the shop. I thought I'd give you a ride home."

"I'll take her," Jericho said.

Kate turned to look at Jericho who eyed Eric. His tone brooked no disagreement.

Eric leaned in and whispered in Kate's ear. ''Watch out for those claws.''

Kate hit Eric in the shoulder and he turned and went down the stairs.

''What was that all about?''

''Nothing.''

''Hmm. Communication between partners?''

''Right. Jericho, you really don't have to take me. I'm going home to change then come back to attend the autopsy.''

''I'll take you home, and I'll bring you back.''

''But it's late.''

''I don't mind. I think we have something to discuss.''

With those ominous words, Kate stepped onto the stairs with Jericho close on her heels.

JERICHO STOOD TOO CLOSE to her while she opened her door. He knew he was crowding her, but he couldn't seem to help himself.

She glanced at him, a flash of irritation in those blue eyes. He was batting a thousand with this woman. First she discovers that he's been interested in her but has hidden it. Then he has to tell the police to arrest a man she's obviously very fond of. But all that seemed to pale in comparison to his attraction to her. He admired the way she had stood up for Danny Hamilton with such passion in her voice when she proclaimed his innocence.

Unfortunately, it didn't make Danny any less suspect. He had a feeling that when the candlestick was tested, the blood on it would match Mrs. LePlante's.

She got the door open and they walked inside. She flipped on a switch and twin lights that sat on hardwood end tables flashed on. Her apartment was beautiful, somewhat on the ornate side, but he liked the Queen Anne style. The sofa was a soft powder blue with a hardwood coffee table that matched the end tables.

In the corner was a beautiful antique baby grand piano. His hands itched to touch the keys. Law would always be his first love, but music came a very close second.

In the dining room sat a small round table and chairs, along with an antique cabinet that held delicate china.

There were landscape paintings on the walls in blues and greens, complementing the throw rugs on the floors. The kitchen was tidy and all the cabinets were painted in white.

"What do you know about Ken Mitchell?"

The question caught him off guard. "Why?"

"He showed up at the crime scene tonight."

"For what reason?"

"He wanted to know when he could clean and rent the apartment again."

"Mercenary."

Kate nodded. "Cold-blooded came to mind."

"Ken's father is a big donator to my campaign."

"He is?"

"In fact, he has given quite a bit of money to the city to help with the homeless. He's huge on charity."

"Well, I'm afraid his son doesn't have as big a heart. I don't even think Mrs. LePlante was cold yet."

"Look, Kate, you're not a homicide detective. It's not your responsibility to work this case. You collect evidence and process it. You need to be objective, and you need to keep emotions out of it."

"Are you saying that I won't do my job?"

"No..."

"Because if you are, you're off the mark."

"You might be too close to this one. Because this is personal, you're letting your feelings come in to play."

"Danny's innocent. That's not emotion. That's a gut instinct."

"My goal is clear, Kate. Get killers off the street. We're on the same side. I have to do my job. I want a report of your findings as soon as it's available."

"You'll get it."

"Danny had motive, means and opportunity, and I've got to prosecute him to the fullest extent of the law."

"This isn't about you," Kate said moving in on him, her sultry scent making him lose his train of thought. It made him crazy, but he couldn't seem to concentrate when this woman got too close to him.

"This is about Danny. All avenues have to be investigated before I will be satisfied. If you don't like it, you can kiss my ass."

There was a buzzing in his ears and he thought it might be a warning signal, but he couldn't seem to think. His hands reached out and enfolded her into his arms, as he lowered his mouth to hers with a soft moan.

His system overloaded, his pulse heavy, his heart laboring against it. He was so sure if she pulled away from him, he would cease to exist. The sensation was like being absorbed into a heated vortex where he was lost. The sheer material of her dress seemed paper-thin as if they touched skin to skin. She moaned and he hardened behind the zipper of his expensive tux pants.

Jericho slid his fingers into her hair, cupping the side of her head as he deepened the kiss. Kate made a helpless sound and opened her mouth. Jericho slipped his tongue inside in a deep, searching kiss.

Gathering her up in a hard, enveloping embrace,

he drew her between his thighs, working his mouth hungrily against hers, pressing her hips even closer. Jericho knew that Kate was capable of this response. It made him feel powerful when she cried out softly, her hands feverishly tugging at his jacket.

Jericho caught her by the hips and molded her flush against him, his mouth wide and hot as he tugged the zipper of her enticing dress down the satin skin of her back. He emitted a low sound of approval when he pulled the dress off her shoulders and encountered nothing but bare skin. He slid his hand up her bare torso, cupping her breast, stroking her with his thumb. She was softer than he could have imagined. Her skin vibrant against his hands alive, so alive.

His touch made her gasp, and she released a shuddering, helpless sound against his mouth. It was sudden, the wrenching of his gut.

He broke the kiss to look down at her. The full breasts tipped with pink nipples hardened into rosy nubs. He used his hands under her arms to arch her back until his mouth engulfed first one sweet tip then the other.

She tasted like nothing he'd ever had. Sweet, pure fire burned his mouth, raged inside him until he let go of her nipple.

She gasped when his gaze collided with hers, her lips parting in pleasure. He brought her lips closer to his, watching the way her eyes glazed when she looked at his mouth. His mouth covered hers urgently, a burst of heat zinging through him startling in its intensity.

And he couldn't imagine ever wanting to kiss another woman as he was kissing Kate. The danger and intensity of his bonding with Kate would be like nothing he'd ever experienced before.

He felt on the brink of miracles and certain disaster.

4

"No," SHE SAID SOFTLY as he tried to strip the dress off her.

She pulled out of his arms and turned away, quickly slipping back into the dress. She backed away from him.

"Kate…" he pleaded, taking a step toward her.

She shook her head, holding her hand out. "No, you teased me for a long time. I told you that you have to wait."

Jericho gritted his teeth and ran his hands through his hair. "Let me explain about that."

"No." She shook her head emphatically. "I don't want to hear any explanations yet. It'll make me weak and I don't want to be weak right now."

"You said you wanted to have sex with me."

"I do."

"Then why not now?"

"Because I call the shots and I say not right now."

Jericho took a deep breath to bring his passion under control. "Okay, you call the shots."

Kate smiled at him in a very unnerving way. "It's nice to know that you're not letting your emotions free rein."

She disappeared into her bedroom and slammed the door.

She'd told him, he thought as he stood there in surprise, his hard-on pulsing behind his zipper.

KATE KNELT ON THE CARPET watching Jericho sleep. Thick dark lashes lay against his bronzed skin. She noted the dark circles beneath those lashes and remembered his words the night before. He wasn't sleeping well because of her. A thrill of excitement tingled down her spine at that admission.

He had dropped her off and she'd suggested that he wait in her office. No one should have to go through an autopsy unless they really had to. When she got back from the autopsy, this is how she found him, asleep on her office couch.

Her eyes roamed over his face and she sighed with the sheer joy of just watching him when that intense gaze was shuttered. Asleep, the force that was so much a part of him was dormant. She could still see it in the lines around his sensual lips, in the proud nose and powerful compelling beauty of his face. Jericho was not like other men she'd met in her life. Maybe that was why she was drawn to him despite his silver-spoon look.

He'd loosened the bow tie and it lay against his stark-white shirt. Here and there the studs had popped open while he'd slept, revealing patches of smooth, supple skin. His cuffs were undone, the gold cuff links with his initials—JSJ—hung loosely from the stitched buttonholes. Worried he would lose them, she reached out and snagged them, dropping them into the pocket of her jeans.

His presence never ceased to cause a stir in a room. Women would follow him with their eyes, desiring all that lightly restrained masculine energy. He prowled, and when he moved, women were compelled to watch, seeing in him qualities that spoke of the best of the species.

There were many more compelling attributes in Jericho other than his mind-drugging good looks and his finely formed body. Regardless of the toughness he showed in court, she suspected he hid a sensitivity that he guarded like a fortress. A sensitivity that had shone through when he'd touched her arm during Danny's interrogation; a sensitivity that came through each time he looked at her. It seduced and lured her, and was as powerful and engaging as his personality.

Even in sleep the lines of his face were taut, as if he struggled in his dreams. His face shadowed with dark brown stubble looked sexy on him. He jerked in his sleep and moaned softly.

The sound cut through her, arrowing to her groin as though it was shot from a bow.

The male scent of him was thick in her nostrils and she breathed deep, irresistibly drawn closer. Her eyes traveled down to his abdomen, bared by his restless slumber, the waistband of his briefs, starkly white against the deep bronze thickness of his stomach muscles and…she looked closer…black lines?

How she wanted to touch his skin, wanted to see what that waistband hid, wanted to put her lips on his skin. All of a sudden, she was beginning to wonder who was enticing who.

"Get as close as you want, Kate."

She gasped. Her eyes flew to his, heavy-lidded and filled with passion. She blushed deeply and furiously to be caught staring at him so obviously.

To hide her embarrassment, she rubbed the back of her neck. "I'm finished with the M.E."

"Cause of death?"

"Manual strangulation."

"So it wasn't the blow?"

"No. It was just a glancing blow with no real force behind it."

"You look beat," he said.

"I am. I don't want to make any mistakes, so I'd better get home and get to bed."

His very brown eyes veiled beneath his tangled chocolate lashes caressed her face, the heightened color on her cheeks. He reached out and ran the back of his hand down her cheek. "Sorry about the 'look closer' comment. It was a response to my very intense and vivid dream of you riding me."

"Are those the only kinds of dreams you have of me?" She looked away from the blatant look in his eyes and wished she hadn't. His shirt still rode up, the taut thick-ridged muscle of his stomach enticing her fingers. If it was his body she was interested in, why did she care so much about his dreams?

"My dreams are uncontrollable, part of my subconscious. Wouldn't it be more important to know what I think when I'm awake?"

"What makes you think I care what you think about me at all?"

"You were just looking at me as if you wanted to devour me. I can only wonder at what you're thinking. The female mind is so intricate, so beautifully complicated."

"And men aren't complicated."

"No, we're not. I want to be inside you. That's a fact and if you need evidence to back that up…"

She couldn't help it. Her eyes fell to his groin and the enticing glimpse of that black ink. Did he have a tattoo there? Jericho the straitlaced, dedicated deputy district attorney didn't seem loose enough to get a tattoo.

Games were never Kate's strong suit. Especially

games where the rules weren't defined or were hidden. Jericho was good at games, mind games, sexual games, word games. She'd seen him in court enough to know that the man could talk circles around anyone and make them think exactly what he wanted them to think. When it came to him, she felt as if she needed to deal with him on a basic level.

She reached out and cupped him in her hand. He was hard and hot. She raised her eyes to his. They were filled with shocked pleasure as if this was the last thing he'd expected her to do. ''That's some hefty evidence there. Maybe I need to examine it.''

She squeezed and stroked up the length of him. Pleasure washed over his expression as his eyes slid closed and he moaned softly in his throat.

It was a difficult thing to want to make this man suffer. The more she teased him, the more she ached. She wanted to feel that hard, hot flesh against her bare hand, run her palm over the silky tip, take him into her mouth and use her tongue on him.

Thoughts came swirling out of the deep recesses of her mind. Decadent thoughts that were alien to her. Something stirred inside her, something dark and needy. It tingled in the tips of her hardened nipples, rippled along her skin, sunk deep into the folds of her groin.

Something that had slumbered unaware until now.

But he'd known all along about her secret desire.

It irked her, making the anger slam into her again. She let go of him. "Did it make you feel powerful to know that I wanted you?"

He opened his eyes and gave a quick shake of his head.

Her breath caught in her throat. "Yet, you pretended not to notice me at all."

"Kate. I wanted you. I've wanted you for a long time…"

"But you didn't do anything about it. Did you? Now I feel like a fool."

She stood up abruptly. "You make me crazy."

"Kate…"

He got off the couch so quickly that she didn't have time to step back.

"It wasn't my intention to make you feel like a fool."

"What was your intention?"

"To keep our relationship professional. I didn't think it would be smart to give in to my baser needs. We work together."

"So all you're interested in is sex, too?"

"I think that if we give in, we can get back to normal."

"Slake our desire?"

"Right."

"That's fine."

Slanting her a look filled with resignation, he inquired, "You're enjoying this, aren't you, Kate?"

"As a matter of fact, I am. Very much."

When he raised his hand to drag it through his hair, the cuff slid down, revealing the strong, bronzed skin of his forearm. The movement also pulled the tailored shirt away from his body and she glimpsed hard, muscled ribs before his hand fell and her view was cut off. Something spiraled inside her tight and warm.

Kate dragged her gaze away from his face. She took a deep breath. "The M.E. said he'd have his report for you tomorrow afternoon."

Jericho took a deep breath as well and started to fasten the studs on his shirt.

"Like I said, I'll start the DNA process tomorrow, since it's getting pretty late."

"I feel guilty for sacking out on you," Jericho said, shrugging into his tuxedo jacket.

"Don't. I appreciate the ride."

HE PULLED UP in front of Kate's building. She held out her hand and it connected with his chest.

She snatched it away as if she'd burned it. "There's no need for you to walk me up. You must be exhausted."

"I'm the one who slept on the couch while you

were working and I insist on walking you up to your apartment.''

She sighed and got out of the car and he followed her into the building and up to her door.

She fitted the key in the lock and turned to him. ''Thanks.''

''Aren't you going to let me in for a moment, Kate?''

She bit her lip and asked, ''Why?''

''I'd like to talk to you and I don't want to do it in the hall.''

She reluctantly moved into her apartment. He followed and closed the door.

He reached out and with his thumb very lightly brushed her lush bottom lip. Such hot desire gripped him that he had to close his eyes to control himself before he could speak again.

With his voice thick and husky, he said, ''How long are you going to be mad at me?'' He brushed at her hair with the back of his hand.

''I don't know,'' she said breathlessly.

He looked away. ''It wasn't personal, Kate. It was because we worked together.'' His voice wasn't convincing. Even he could hear it.

She gazed up at him, her eyes such a clear blue-gray glistening with skepticism. He wanted those eyes full of desire for him, knowing himself to be insane, but he was tired of fighting himself.

''What's the other reason?''

Working with her day in and day out was like walking a tightrope with no net. Then having to face her in her newfound sexuality was wearing at his self-control. It was harder and harder for him to keep his hands off her. His body wanted her, craved intimate contact with that soft, velvet skin.

''I'm afraid that if I start touching you, wanting you, I won't be able to stop,'' he murmured.

She blinked up at him, a fire igniting in her eyes.

He leaned toward her, his thumb moving across her jaw with deliberate slowness, savoring the way she felt against his skin. ''Like silk,'' he whispered against her ear before his eyes lowered to her mouth. He just stood there, his thumb brushing along her jawbone.

His other hand came up, his thumb gently sliding across the back of her hand and around to her wrist.

She swayed toward him and he breathed deeply. Discovering how much Kate wanted him hadn't been a good thing. Although the wild side of him howled at the thought, the rational part was convinced that he would have taken her against his desk long ago if he'd realized the extent of her passion.

''Tell me,'' he coaxed. ''Tell me how much you want me.''

She made a small sound in her throat and shook her head.

"Come on, Katie."

Somehow his shirt studs had come undone. With his foot he shut the apartment door.

The silence stretched out as he pulled her toward him, very deliberately pressing her palm to his bare chest. "Tell me what you want to do to me," he sighed raggedly.

She leaned into him, placing her cheek against his chest and refusing to speak. "Okay. I'll tell you what I want. It's you. You tantalize me. I wonder things, things that make me hard with desire."

She slid her palm along the sleek muscles, making a small heated sound. The sweet husky noise teemed with need and excitement.

He closed his eyes against that small murmur. His fingers tightened on her wrist, stopping her exploration, just holding her hand against him.

"Little witch," he moaned in a voice laced with a combination of denial and desire.

Slowly, as if in a dream, she raised her hand to gently touch his cheek. And like the witch he named her, enchantment flowed from her through that gentle touch. Warmth spread with gentle probing fingers, seeking out the coldest, deepest part of his soul, filling it with light.

He closed his eyes to better concentrate on the way her hand felt against him. "Have you wanted to touch me?" he demanded hoarsely.

"Yes, forever," she whispered, her hands traveling over the contours beneath her probing fingers.

Kate's hands on his chest felt like two fiery brands burning his skin. He was burning up with need.

Her hand moved down his torso, running over the ridges of muscles along his ribs to the thick, seriated muscle of his abdomen.

When she reached the waistband of his slacks, she tucked her fingers inside and ran them around.

She groaned heatedly and the sound of it skated along his nerve endings like quicksilver igniting pleasure centers.

With a quick, lithe movement, he grabbed her hands and twined them around his neck. He jerked her against him with such power that the force of it wrung a cry of surprise out of her. Without giving her a chance to even think, his lips descended to hers, fiery and demanding, as if his very life depended on her response.

Her breath was dammed in her lungs and the hard pressure of his mouth sent delicious sensations to pool with hot tingles in her lower body.

She wanted more, yet felt as if she couldn't possibly get close enough to him. She was aware of the hardness of his big, strong body and she wanted to explore every muscled inch.

His hand slid over her buttocks, holding her in

place as he pushed against her softness, kneading the firm curves while he pulled her tighter to him. And Kate stilled suddenly, her breath caught between breathing in and breathing out as she felt the hot, rigid length of him pressed against her clothed hips.

Unable to help herself, her hands went to the part of him that was quintessentially male. With the flat of her hand, she pressed against him, then cupped him, squeezing gently. It was so arousing to touch a man like this. To take him like this. She hoped she wasn't being clumsy.

A full-throated grown escaped Jericho's lips as he abruptly stopped moving. Kate could feel the coiled need in him as he strained to hold on to his self-control. She felt the quivers throughout his body as he tried to master his raging desire, and she felt him lose the battle with himself. He gripped her buttocks tighter and drove himself upward, grinding his hips against her hands and stomach.

''Jericho,'' she breathed. Kate had had sex before, but Jericho made her feel inept. Beneath her innocence pulsed the need to be filled by this man.

His hand closed around her breast, his thumb brushing over the nipple. Kate felt as though she was going to come out of her skin.

He wrapped his arms around her and whirled, setting her on the edge of her writing desk. His eyes captured hers, a glittering light so full of stark desire for her that it made Kate groan.

He pulled her T-shirt over her head, forgetting her protests as his warm hands caressed her through the lace of her bra. She arched her back instinctively giving all that she had.

He filled his hands with the soft weight of her exquisite flesh; flicking his thumbs over each nipple, liking her soft gasp each time he did it.

"We don't need to wait, Kate."

The words reverberated in her head. And she managed to say, "Jericho, no. Stop. Now."

He convulsed against her, his mouth going back to hers. She could feel the trembling in his hands, his body—or was it her shaking? She couldn't tell.

"What are you saying? Are you teasing me, Kate?"

"Every time you come near me, I lose control." She pushed against his chest. "I told you it's my call." Her breathlessness betrayed her state of arousal.

He braced his hands against the desk and breathed in and out forcefully. "You're kidding?"

She stared at him, still unwavering, and she saw when he believed her.

"I guess the living room would be a little too adventurous for you."

"What is that supposed to mean?"

He did up the studs on his shirt, but left his bow tie loose. "Come on, Kate. You don't seem very adventurous to me. Ask anyone. They'd say the same thing. Cool, calm and collected. Kate always gets the job done."

"You're just trying to goad me because I won't give in. Sounds like sour grapes to me."

"I can wait, Kate. But can you?"

With that he captured her lips and shot sensation through her body like lightning bolts, and all she could do was stand there and absorb the shock. She couldn't move. Couldn't breathe. Whatever it was she had felt building between them hit her a hundred times over.

Her heart slammed into her throat, stayed there while his mouth continued to seduce. She should pull away, she thought hazily. Put distance between herself and this man who had started a war between need and doubt raging inside her.

But she couldn't. Didn't want to. The primal male taste of him was potent, like a dark, seductive dream.

"Jericho…" His name came hoarsely from her throat. "I…" In an open, mindless invitation, she parted her lips beneath his and surrendered.

Swearing, he fisted his hand in her hair, tipped her head back and deepened the kiss. Desire shot like a bullet through her.

Her hands streaked up. She dug her fingers into his hard, muscled upper arms while her senses staggered with the thrill of his touch.

His mouth was a banquet, and she was desperate with hunger. She smelled the inviting scent of him, felt the strength in the arms that held her, heard the thunder of his heart against hers. Sudden, searing need for him edged at her throat.

That need frightened her. It reduced her to a quivering mass, made every logical thought leave her head, had her desperate to lie naked in his arms while they engaged in wild, raging lovemaking.

She pulled her head back, her lungs heaving, her breasts rising and falling against his chest.

"That was a challenge, wasn't it?" Her breath shuddered from beneath her lips.

"Damn right," he agreed, his voice raw.

A scant inch of charged air separated their lips while she tried to think past the ache that had settled inside her. Against hers, his body was strong and hard and tense, and all she wanted was to spend the rest of the night in his arms.

"Time for you to go," she said, even as a shudder of pure longing went through her. "I can hold out if you can."

He smiled and she remembered that he loved competition. That smile cut through her, reminding

her that she was so very far out of her league where
Jericho was concerned.

"And I am too adventurous."

He slid his hands in one long, possessive stroke
down the sides of her body. Then back up. Light
from her lamps slanted across the strong planes of
his face. Desire had turned his eyes the color of
burnt umber.

"Prove it."

She broke eye contact and took a step sideways,
forcing him to drop his hands. "I'll see you tomorrow."

Even now, when her brain could barely function,
she knew that this man had touched something deep
inside her, something that no other man had
touched. And the intensity of those emotions scared
her to death. She wasn't used to chaos, had never
liked the jumble of emotions taking over. She used
her intellect, but it seemed to be lacking in this case.

That knowledge shook her. She had to regain control. Her fingers clenched into fists as she stared up
at him. He looked dangerous. Compelling, reckless.
Dangerous.

And if the man himself wasn't dangerous, what
she felt for him when he kissed her surely was.

She couldn't let herself fall for him. This wasn't
about emotion or the long term. This was about a

souvenir and who could hold out the longest. It was now also, surprisingly, about adventure.

"Tomorrow, Katie."

After her door closed, she sagged against the desk. Dazed, she lifted a hand, touched her fingers to her lips, lips that felt hot and swollen and thoroughly kissed. It took every ounce of her self-control not to pull her door open, go pounding down the stairs and drag him back into her apartment.

5

KATE WOKE UP before her alarm, before the sun had illuminated the horizon. In the still of the morning, as she lay in her bed, she thought about Jericho and his challenge.

She got out of bed feeling troubled and out of sorts. An hour doing yoga had always set her on a good path in the morning.

Kate walked into the spacious kitchen and picked up her diffuser, an electronic bowl with a lid that allowed aromatic oils to be heated, releasing their intoxicating smell into the air to relieve stress.

Her normal routine was to get up and do an hour of yoga to begin the day. She walked into her living room. Just looking at the desk made her heart beat rapidly.

She placed the diffuser on the lip of the fireplace and plugged it in. Automatically, she mixed the oils and then covered the concoction.

In her bedroom, she shucked her pajamas. Putting on a bodysuit, she adjusted the straps for comfort. Kate had been doing yoga since her early teens.

She'd discovered that yoga could give her a measure of inner peace in her hectic life. Where Sienna and Lana preferred more physical activities, Kate liked the quiet wellness that the exercises brought her.

She ran a hand through her hair, coiling it tightly, then pinning the mass to the top of her head. Back in the living room, she pulled out her mat and went through her preliminary exercises.

For an hour she moved through her routine with fluid, graceful movements, feeling the pleasant and stimulating stretch of her muscles. The oils in the diffuser permeated the room with the scent of sandalwood, palma rosa and lemon. Kate breathed deeply through each exercise, and she felt some of the stress from the previous day and night dissipate.

Finally, her routine ended and she sat down on her mat. She placed her hands loosely on her knees and closed her eyes.

But the peace she usually felt at the end of a routine wasn't there. She couldn't grasp it. She breathed evenly and tried to force it, but knew that wasn't going to help.

She opened her eyes and huffed out a breath of frustration. It was what he'd said last night that was bothering her so much.

He was right. She had a good reputation as a forensic scientist, but surely wasn't known for being adventurous.

But she wanted to be. Her fantasies were varied and in them she was bold and wild. One in particular featured Jericho, warm, melted chocolate and her tongue. Why *couldn't* she be that way with Jericho?

Before she invited him to her bed she wanted to equalize the playing field. The best person to help her with that was one person who knew a lot about sex and how to please a man. Paige Dempsey.

Lana's sister owned her own sex toy company and just last year met FBI agent Justin Conner who, believe it or not, had arrested her for fraud. It had all worked out in the end and they were soon to be married. So it was with a little trepidation that Kate paid the taxi driver and walked up the path to Paige's quaint little house.

She knocked and waited patiently. Finally, Justin opened the door.

"Kate? What are you doing here? It's—" he looked at his watch "—seven o'clock." His sleepy eyes widened. "Is Lana okay?"

"Yes, she's fine. I actually came to talk to Paige. Is she up?"

"Not yet, but I'll tell her you're here."

He walked away and disappeared into the bedroom. Five minutes later, Paige came out, tying a robe around her middle. "Hey, Kate," she said, hugging her.

"Hi, Paige. I'm sorry about barging in on you so

early, but it couldn't wait. I won't have time to drop by tonight."

"It's no problem. Want a cup of coffee?" Paige smiled sleepily.

"Sounds great."

After Paige gave Kate a cup of steaming coffee, they sat on the living room couch. Kate looked apprehensively at the bedroom.

"Don't worry, Justin is in the shower. What's up?" Paige asked, taking a sip of her coffee.

"You are aware of our souvenir dare, right?" Unable to sit still, Kate jumped up and began to pace.

"I am, and you guys are crazy, although Sienna and A.J. seem to be very happy. Not to mention Lana and Sean can't keep their eyes and hands off each other. Who is your target?"

"Jericho St. James."

"The guy running for D.A.?"

"Yes."

"Wow. I've seen him on TV. He's gorgeous and I love what he stands for. I'm planning on voting for him. Way to go, Kate."

"I think he might be a little out of my league."

Paige smiled wickedly. "Oh, Kate. No man is out of a woman's league. Are you saying you aren't sure about bedding him?"

"He said I wasn't adventurous."

"So."

"He's right. I'm not. I know who I am, Paige. I've always used my mind to get where I want to go. I thought about going to the bookstore and picking up a book about seduction, but was hoping that you could give me some pointers. I want to knock Jericho on his butt first."

"Uh, before you get your hands on it?"

Kate felt the blood suffuse her face. "Right."

"From what I've seen of our prosecutor, I'd say it's a pretty nice ass."

"Who has a nice ass?" Justin said, coming out of the bedroom.

Kate wanted to crawl under the table.

Paige rose and went to him, curling her arms around his neck and kissing his mouth. "You never mind, mister. This is women's stuff."

Kate saw the way Justin's eyes caressed Paige's face and she wanted Jericho to look at her like that. Really see her the way Justin saw Paige.

Justin left and Paige came back to sit down. "Look, I think you might have it mixed up. The body doesn't govern sex, Kate. The mind does. Sure there are chemical reactions that happen, but it all starts up here." She pointed to her temple.

"Like."

"Take Jericho, for instance. Why do you think he's sexy?"

"He is."

"But pinpoint it." Paige took another leisurely sip, letting Kate think about her answer. "You can't, right. That's because it's a lot of things about him that you find attractive. His mouth?"

"Definitely. And he knows how to use it."

"His mind?"

"Brilliant."

"You see what I'm saying. We could go on and on, but it's still the jumble of intricate things that make him sexy to you. Intellect is always sexy. From your mind comes imagination and you can incorporate what you think into what you do. Seduction is all mind. Believe me."

"I should use my mind to seduce Jericho?"

"Exactly. Seduction requires art, attention to details and a devoted imagination."

"How do I do that?"

"Push his buttons. Give him the promise of what he wants and then, baby, deliver."

"Think about being adventurous and it'll happen?"

"Sure. Go with what you feel, throw caution to the wind and take what you want. Do what you want. I don't know any man who wouldn't appreciate that in a woman."

"I've never been good at that, Paige."

"Why?"

"I don't know."

"Maybe you should think about it, Kate. Maybe then the answer you seek about how to seduce Jericho will come to you. Perhaps it's not his body you want. Maybe you want his mind, too."

"This is a dare and by the very nature of a dare, I have to overcome my fear of following through. It wouldn't be a dare otherwise."

"True but, God, Kate, don't think too much, either. Sex is both a physical and mental thing."

"Thanks, Paige." Kate looked down at her watch. "I've got to go. I really appreciate all you said."

"Go get 'em tiger."

"How DID IT GO with St. James?"

Kate lowered the report she'd been reading, leaned forward and wrinkled her nose at the paper cup Eric had placed in the center of her disordered desk.

"Doesn't look like a Grande Mocha to me."

"It isn't any of that latte crap. It's coffee black and you, my dear, look like you could use it."

She narrowed her eyes at him. "Banner, are you telling me I look like hell?"

"Whoa," he said, putting up his hands. He gave her an engaging grin. "Guess I'd better behave."

"Guess so. I like my latte crap very much, so show some respect." Kate glanced toward the door.

Eric's eyes followed the path of hers. "You didn't answer my question."

"What question," Kate said, looking at the clock and then the door again.

"Expecting someone?"

Startled she looked at him. "No. No one."

"Then why are you so distracted?"

"No reason. Let me fill you in on the analyses I did last night." She hadn't realized that she was waiting for Jericho to walk through the door. He'd said he'd see her. Anticipation curled in her stomach.

"You're ducking the question."

She gave him an annoyed look. "The last time I checked you're neither my nursemaid nor my mommy."

"This is interesting. You've always told me about your love life or lack thereof. Now you're telling me to back the hell off."

"Message received. Now to the analyses."

"Must have been some night." He waited a heartbeat. "Did you sleep with him?"

"You shouldn't anger me, Banner."

"Or worse yet, you didn't."

Kate stared hard at her friend, realizing that he knew her too well. "Eric! Focus. There's really nothing to talk about."

Eric regarded her, shaking his head. "I told you he was too much for you."

Kate blurted, "He's not too much for me and I'll prove it."

"How?" Eric challenged.

She knew he was baiting her, but she couldn't help herself. *All* her friends, including Jericho, thought she was Sister Kate and she was so sick of it. "By doing something adventurous."

"Adventurous? Not a word I would use to describe you."

She narrowed her eyes at him. "What words would you use?"

"Conservative. In control. Sedate."

"Do you know that the synonyms for *sedate* are staid and dull?"

Banner raised his brows. "No. I didn't mean that." He shook his head. "And only you would point that out."

"But that's what you think I am—sedate."

Eric looked contrite. "You do a great job, Kate. That should be enough."

His demeanor didn't satisfy her. She sighed. "Right. Gotcha."

"You're upset?"

She gave him a savage look. "No. Why should I be upset when my co-worker calls me dull and my other friends call me Sister Kate? Why should that bother me at all?''

''There's nothing wrong with being conservative.''

''No. I guess not.''

''Kate…''

She held up her hand. ''Just forget it. We'd better get to work. After all, an innocent man's life is at stake here.''

Eric looked as though he wanted to say more, but he thought better of it. He sat in one of the chairs in front of Kate's desk. ''How can you be sure that Danny didn't commit this murder?''

''I've known Danny for six years. I've lived in that building. Danny couldn't intentionally hurt anyone. He's not a violent man.''

''That may be the key word—intentionally. What if you're wrong?''

She gave Eric a knowing look. ''I'm not. I have a gut feeling about this. I have no doubt that Danny was in her apartment, but I don't think he killed her.''

''Who do you like?''

''I'd rather not say right now because I haven't done enough investigation.''

''Let's get to work then.''

''I thought we should reconstruct the crime scene

and figure out what happened.'' Kate paused and sat back. ''I'd say she was murdered in the bathroom.''

''Why?''

''She was found there. And there'd been a struggle in there—the mirror was broken. I got blood off glass fragments and drops on the sink. My guess is the murderer surprised her somehow.''

''You think the guy was in the bathroom?''

''Yes.''

''While Hamilton was there?'' Eric mused.

''That's what I think. Mrs. LePlante had her argument with Danny in the kitchen. Danny got agitated and left and went into the living room to get out the door. If Danny had strangled her, he would have cuts on his hands.''

''What makes you think he'd try to leave?''

''Danny doesn't like confrontation. He'll do almost anything to avoid it.''

''Including hitting someone with a candlestick?'' Eric asked skeptically.

''If he felt threatened, then yes I think he would lash out.''

Eric nodded. ''Okay, go ahead.''

''I think Danny hit Mrs. LePlante with the candlestick and knocked her down here.'' Kate had done a rough sketch of the murder scene in her notebook. She flipped it open and pointed to the spot where they found traces of blood. ''There was blood found on the carpet and I'd say it's Mrs. LePlante's. She touched her temple and left the bloody hand-print there, got up and went to the bathroom to clean it up and bandage it, or may have decided to check it out in the mirror. Mmm. The mirror is right in front of the shower. If someone had been hiding there, she might have seen him.''

"You think someone was hiding in the shower?" Eric said, looking at the sketch.

"I do. I found some hair and fiber evidence there. Not many people wear clothes in the shower."

"So she sees him and then what happens?" He handed the notebook back to her.

"She turns and tries to run from the bathroom, but he catches her near the door and slams her against the full-length mirror. It breaks, he cuts himself and he strangles Mrs. LePlante."

"Why?"

"That part I don't know. Either it's someone who hates her or he was there for a reason."

"Robbery?"

"Possibly. But I always thought of strangulation as a very personal crime. Putting your hands on the victim and all, getting satisfaction out of squeezing the life out of her. We'll know more when Mrs. LePlante's daughter has had time to go through her things."

"Is this what you're going to give to Sanders, Parker and St. James?"

"Yes, once I've had time to analyze the blood and the fingerprints."

Eric rose. "Let's get on that now."

They went out into the lab to the computer. "I digitized the fingerprints that we lifted from the candlestick, the kitchen, the bedroom and the bathroom."

"Have you tried to match them to the suspect and the victim yet?"

"No." Kate sat at the computer and pulled up the file with the most prominent fingerprint. "There were a few fingerprints on the candlestick, some were obscured, but I got two good ones."

"I have the fingerprint for Danny Hamilton that was taken when he was booked," Eric said, setting the print into the scanner.

Kate split the screen. She looked at her watch. "This is going to take about sixty minutes. Why don't you go to lunch?"

"How about you?"

"I have one more thing to do, then I'll go."

"Okay. See you."

Kate went over to her workstation and picked up a piece of rope. For another case, she needed to see if a victim had committed suicide by tying her own hands behind her back.

The door to the lab opened and Kate was glad that Eric hadn't left for lunch, yet. She said without turning around, "Great. I need to tie your hands behind your back."

"Then what are you going to do to me?"

Jericho's deep voice set up reverberations so penetrating they seemed to liquefy her bones. She whipped around to find him standing in her lab.

How did he do it? Every time she looked at him, he took her breath away. He was dressed in a blue suit with tiny pinstripes of red. It was impeccably cut and tailored to his awesome frame. He was wearing a red tie and stark white shirt. He looked sharp and dangerous and oh so sexy.

She wished she could think of something equally sexy to say, but her mind was a blank.

"What are you doing here?"

"I came to check your progress."

"That's different."

"Why?"

"You rarely come to the lab. Whenever I have my reports, I go to you."

"True, so I came because I wanted to see you. Sue me."

"I doubt I would win."

He smiled and moved closer to her, looking down at the rope. "I don't mind being a guinea pig if you need help."

Kate had totally forgotten what she had been about to ask Eric to do.

"Could you turn around?"

He did as she asked and she took a deep breath when her eyes fell to his broad shoulders. "Hands behind your back."

He complied and she studied them, big, competent and often gentle when they touched her. She slipped the rope around his wrist and duplicated the knots that had been around the victim's wrist. She visualized each loop as she made it, finally convinced at the end of the experiment that the victim of possible suicide couldn't have completed tying the ropes herself.

She turned to the phone and picked it up and dialed Sanders. "Tom. I've just completed my review of the knots for the Jody Christiansen case. I would say that she couldn't have done it herself."

"Murder?"

"Yes. I'll have my report on your desk this afternoon."

"Thanks, Kate."

When she dropped the phone back in the cradle, Jericho was standing there with his hands tied behind his back. It was an intriguing position for him to be in and made her feel just a tad more in control.

"Are you going to untie me?"

"Of course," she said as she spun him around

and took off the rope. "Sorry about that," she said as he rubbed his wrists. "I get carried away when I make a discovery like that. I don't want Tom to waste a minute."

"It's good to see that you're dedicated to your job, even when you leave your boss tied up."

"Does that mean a good evaluation next time?"

"A plus." He grinned.

It was the first time that he'd ever done that. First time she'd noticed how sexy it was with those soft crinkles at the corners of his eyes. He'd laughed and he'd smiled, but he had never grinned at her. It transformed him and made him less intimidating.

His grin faded and his eyes traveled over her face and down her body. She fought the urge to adjust the hip-hugging black skirt, wondering at her bravado in pairing it with the georgette black shirt that showed a lot more of her black bra than she would have ever thought to do. But Lana had been persuasive when she'd insisted that this attire was perfectly fine for daywear.

She'd been right. No one else had even batted an eyelash and she'd gotten compliments on her clothing.

Kate dropped the rope out of her nerveless fingers at the soft gleam in his eyes. She bent to retrieve it and her heavy hair cascaded over her shoulders.

Straightening, she placed the rope on the lab table behind her.

He reached out and snagged the loose strands. Threading the gleaming ends though his fingers, he said, ''When was the last time you cut your hair?''

''I can't remember,'' she replied, her breath damming in her lungs as she watched him rub her hair between his thumb and first two fingers. ''So silky.''

Just then the door banged open and Eric entered. Jericho dropped her hair.

Eric stopped when he saw Jericho. ''Jericho,'' he said by way of greeting. Then he said to her, ''I've got a lot to do so I brought my lunch back here, thought you might need a hand with the fingerprint.''

''Lunch?'' Jericho said, turning back to her. ''I'm sorry that I kept you from eating.''

''It's all right.''

''No. It isn't. Let me buy you lunch.''

''The fingerprint.''

''It's still scanning,'' Eric said. ''Go ahead. I'll call you on your cell phone when it's done.''

She gave Eric a lethal look, but he just smiled at her. ''Thanks, Banner. I owe you one.''

''No need to thank me.''

Jericho eyed her during the exchange. With a last look toward Eric, he ushered her out the door.

"What's going on with Banner?"

"Nothing, he just likes to rib me about you."

"He's not interested in you…right?"

"Eric? No."

"Good."

That brought a smile to her lips. She liked that Jericho was asking. It meant he was very interested in her and felt proprietary. She thought that was very good.

"Where do you usually eat lunch?"

"At my desk."

He sighed. "When you go out."

"Across the street at the deli."

They came out of the lab building and quickly crossed the street. Jericho ordered pastrami on rye and Kate got her usual ham and cheese. They went back outside and sat at one of the tables.

"Do you work through your lunch hour often?"

"I don't mean to. I just lose track of time and before I know it, it's six or seven."

"You shouldn't go so long without eating. It's not good for you."

"You sound like my mother."

"She's right."

Kate unwrapped her sandwich, but her appetite was nonexistent. "She means well, but my mother hasn't ever really understood me. My father, either."

"Why is that?" He took a bite of his sandwich.

"I was always asking questions. I excelled in school and they truly just didn't know how to interact with me. I think they thought some alien must haven taken their baby and placed me there instead."

"They must have been proud of you when you went off to college."

She played with the wrapper. "I think they were more relieved. I didn't go out much. I was more interested in studying and reading."

"And science."

"Lord, yes." She smiled. It was something that she felt comfortable with. It never made her do or feel anything she didn't want. "I entered every science fair."

"And won?"

"Of course, why else enter a contest if you don't intend to win. What's the point?"

"Those are my thoughts exactly."

She studied him and smiled. "If you're talking about our challenge, then you're going to be disappointed. I'll win, Jericho."

He reached out and captured her hand. Turning it over, he gently caressed her palm. "What makes you think you won't give in first?"

"Pure determination." It took all her concentration to speak. ''Mind over matter. I'm very good at that. What are you good at?'' she threw at him.

''Making you scream out in gut-clenching, heart-stopping pleasure.''

6

"GOOD ANSWER," Kate said, her eyes widening.

"I've got a bargain for you."

"Yeah, what?"

"I'll break the rules for you. Give me a week and I'll bring out the passionate woman in you."

"What do you want from me?"

"Heat, Kate. I want to see that hot woman in you."

"After that, things will go back to normal and we'll be boss and co-worker again?" she asked, finally picking up her sandwich and taking a bite.

He nodded.

Kate's cell phone rang. She chewed quickly and wiped her mouth before she spoke. "Quinn. I'll be back over in a minute. Thanks." She closed her phone. "The fingerprints are done. We can go have a look now."

He grabbed her arm. "What do you say?"

"Okay. I'll agree to that, but you have to give me something in return."

He narrowed his eyes at her and said, "What?"

"I want a souvenir from you when this is all over. You see, my two friends and I made a pact. We each had to seduce a man and get a souvenir because we're women who dare."

Jericho suddenly understood why it was so important to Kate to be the one in charge. This dare dictated that she become a daring woman, but her fear still held her back. He could cut her some slack. He wanted that daring woman very much. "It's a deal."

They got up and crossed the street. "There is something else that you're good at, Jericho."

They entered the building and he stopped near the doorway to the stairs. "What's that?"

"You're absolutely amazing in court, riveting. I can't keep my eyes off you or stop my heart from beating fast. It's very exciting."

The praise coming from her made him warm inside, a place that craved soft, sweet words from this woman. He grabbed her arm and dragged her into the stairwell. She made a little squeak as he hauled her through the door. He pressed her back against the wall.

"This is insane," she managed to say.

But he saw the desire in her eyes and it spoke to him. Then his mouth closed over hers.

She didn't push him away. For nearly one heartbeat, he was lost, paralyzed, struck deaf, dumb and blind. In a tidal wave, every sense flooded back, every nerve snapped, every pulse jolted.

Her mouth was soft, as were her hands as they delved into his hair, as was her body. He felt terrifyingly, gloriously masculine pressed against her. A need he hadn't been aware of exploded into bloom. His briefcase hit the floor with a thud as she wrapped herself around him.

He was no longer thinking. A man would starve to death after only one taste. A man would certainly beg for more. She was soft and strong and sinfully sweet, with a flavor that both tempted and tormented.

Heat radiated between them as the sauna-like air sealed their kiss. The din of nearby street noises, horns and tires sounded around them, along with her dazed, throaty moan.

He pulled back once to look at her face, saw himself in the cornflower-blue eyes, and then his mouth crushed hers again.

No, this wasn't going to be a one-time deal.

He pulled back again, staggered by what had ripped through him in so short a time. He was winded, weak and the sensation infuriated as much as baffled him. She only stood there, staring at him with a mixture of shock and hunger in her eyes.

"Are you crazy? Anyone could have seen us."

"I know."

''Cops use these stairs and my co-workers.''

''I know.''

''But you didn't care?''

''No. Not at that moment.''

Voices echoed in the stairwell and Kate extricated herself quickly and started down the stairs. He followed her, wanting to reach out to capture her tumbling hair. He was disappointed that she'd bolted. He knew there was a daring woman inside her, longing to get out. He wanted that woman.

But he understood her more than she knew. It was hard to let yourself feel, once you'd stuffed it so deep inside that you're afraid you couldn't find it again.

He'd done that when he'd worked at his uncle's law firm and saw the inequities every day until he couldn't stomach it anymore. Now in court, he could let his passion show. He could do something about the lying scumbags who filed through his courtroom on a daily basis. People like Danny Hamilton who were too cowardly to admit to what they had done. Hiding behind his handicap wasn't going to save him. He could get to the truth by digging as deep and as long as he wanted.

And he intended to prove that Danny Hamilton killed Marie LePlante.

THE MAN WAS INSANE. That was the only explanation for kissing her like that in the stairwell. And she was skirting along the sanity line herself. She'd lost herself there in the stairwell. She hadn't been able to breathe. For the first time in her memory, she could do nothing but feel. And the feelings had come so fast, so sharp and strong, they'd left her in tatters.

She wanted to get these fingerprints read and to get Jericho out of her work space before she did something completely foolish.

Eric was standing next to the computer screen, leaving the chair open for her. Kate sat and looked closely at the fingerprints. Her heart sank.

"Do they match?" Jericho asked.

"Yes. Danny touched the candlestick."

Jericho put his hand briefly on her shoulder and squeezed. She turned to look up at him and the compassion in his eyes made her want to curl up in his arms.

Danny had his hand on the candlestick. There was no mistaking the print that was taken when he was booked and the one that was lifted from the metal of the candlestick. She would have sworn on a stack of bibles that Danny couldn't hurt anyone. Ever. It shook her resolve. So Mrs. LePlante may have been struck with the candlestick, but that didn't mean that Danny had strangled the woman in her own bathroom.

Why would Danny hit her in the first place? It didn't make sense to Kate. Danny was a gentle soul. She'd seen him pick up a stray kitten once and he'd been as gentle as a child. What could have led him to pick up the candlestick and hit Mrs. LePlante?

The answers to those questions could come from only one source. Danny himself. Kate needed to talk to him.

"I'll get this information to Parker and Sanders," Eric said as he exited with copies of the prints.

"This pretty much seals Danny's guilt," Jericho said.

"Mrs. LePlante didn't die from the blow."

"No. True. She died from strangulation."

"It doesn't prove that Danny strangled her."

"Kate. Danny had means, motive and opportunity. I can make a case on the witness who saw him fighting with Mrs. LePlante on numerous occasions, heard him arguing with her that night. He was at her apartment at the right time she died. The coroner confirmed that last night."

"I still don't think he's capable of killing anyone."

"Even someone he hates?"

Kate leaned forward, jaw set, eyes narrowed. "No. Not even then," she said vehemently.

"It's time to close this case."

"But I still haven't analyzed the glass evidence, the fibers in the shower and the blood."

"I don't want you to waste time on this case. Move on."

"Even if an innocent man's life is at stake?"

"Kate, they're rarely innocent. It's a sad fact, but it's true."

Jericho's cell phone rang and he pulled the instrument off his hip. "I'll be right there." He looked down at her. "I've got to go."

She shook her head and turned to stare at the computer screen. Facts were never wrong and this one was extremely damaging. Kate knew she wasn't wrong. She seldom was. That was fact. Although she would have to admit that challenging Jericho to a match of wills might have been a bad idea.

The man played to win. Why, oh, why, had she agreed to this souvenir dare? She wasn't as brave as she thought she was and surely not as brave as she wanted to be.

Something shivered along her skin. Something elusive and out of reach. Would he make her rise to the challenge and if and when she did, how would that feel, how would she deal with those feelings, and what would she do if they got out of control?

THE CLANG OF THE CELL at her back was loud in the air as she faced Danny.

"Miss Kate! I'm so happy to see you. Did you

come to get me out?'' He threw his arms around her and hugged her tight.

"No, Danny, I'm sorry I didn't, but I've come to visit you and see how you are doing. Is everyone treating you all right?'' She hugged him back tightly.

"I guess so. It's scary in here especially at night.'' He sat on the cot and Kate sat next to him.

She put her hand on his arm and smiled. "How about I go to your apartment and get something of yours for you?''

Danny nodded enthusiastically and clapped his hands together. "Yes. That would be very good. You're a kind lady.''

"Danny, do you know what's going to happen tomorrow?''

"No. Not really.''

"You're going to have to talk to the judge. It's called your arraignment. You will be informed of the charges, advised of your rights, and the consequences of your plea and asked to enter a plea. Do you know what a plea is?''

"No.''

"You will tell the judge that you're not guilty.''

"I'm not. I didn't kill Mrs. LePlante.''

"Just tell him you're not guilty. You don't have to say anything else.''

"Will you be there?"

"Yes, Danny, I will." She squeezed his arm. "Now before you plea, the judge is going to inform you of your rights. You have the right to confront any witnesses."

"Confront?"

"Yes, if someone says something about you, you have the right to say whether that is true or not," she told him gently.

He frowned and said, "Oh. Some people get mad when you tell them they're wrong."

"I know, Danny, but you won't have to talk to the witnesses. Your attorney will talk to them for you."

"Good. I don't like yelling."

"The judge will also tell you that you have a right to a speedy jury trial. You have the right not to incriminate yourself."

"I don't know some big words."

"Like incriminate?"

"Yes. That's a big word."

"Incriminate means that you don't have to tell your side of the story if it will show that you are guilty."

"So I can lie silently."

She smiled at his naiveté. "Sort of, Danny."

"But I'm not lying."

"Then you have nothing to worry about." Kate

smiled to reassure him. "Danny, I need to ask you a question. Did you hit Mrs. LePlante?"

Danny ducked his head and refused to meet her eyes. "She was a mean lady."

"I know. But did you hit her?"

Danny's face contorted and he covered his face. Kate's stomach clenched. She put her arm around his shoulders.

"You can tell me, Danny. Did you hit her?"

"Yes, but I didn't mean to. She was yelling at me because there was water all over her floor and she was expecting her daughter for dinner. I didn't do anything wrong when I fixed the sink. She shoved something too hard against the pipes and it made a leak. She tried to blame it on me. She told me that she was going to tell Mr. Mitchell that I was good for nothing. I tried to leave, but she wouldn't stop. She wouldn't get out of my way. So I hit her and I ran when she fell."

"Was there anyone else in the apartment?"

"No, she was just coming home from the store and she was running late, she said. She called me on the phone and made me come to her apartment. Her face was red because she was really mad."

"You're absolutely sure no one else was there?"

"Not that I saw. I was trying to get away from her."

"Were you ever in her bathroom?"

"No. I didn't like working there very much, so I tried to do her jobs fast."

"So she never had any bathroom problems and you were never in there?"

"No. Never. Can I go home now?"

"No, not yet, Danny. I'm going to call a friend of mine to help you. His name is Stephen Castle and he's a very good defense attorney."

"Thank you, Miss Kate. You won't forget to bring something from my place, will you?"

"I won't forget, Danny. I'll come back to see you soon."

As she stepped out of the cell, she knew that handling Danny's case wasn't a good idea. It could really mess up Jericho's prosecution, but she knew in her heart that Danny wasn't responsible for Mrs. LePlante's death. She was going to prove it.

She had no doubt that Stephen would handle Danny's case. Another violation against her sworn duty as a criminalist in service to San Diego, but she also couldn't go against her conscience that dictated to her that if she turned her back on Danny right now, he'd be convicted of the LePlante murder and be sent to prison. She couldn't let that happen to him, no matter what the repercussions meant to her job or her personal life.

Danny was all alone and had nobody to look out for him. That left her and if she buckled under the pressure of her job or Jericho's orders against what she believed, who would that make her?

Not anyone she would like at all.

IT WASN'T WHAT she'd expected, Kate thought as she ascended the stairs leading to the two-story brownstone's front porch. The beds of begonias and marigolds that lined his walk surprised her. Jericho didn't seem the type to notice small things like flowers. The wooden swing hanging by chains from the porch was also a surprise. Relaxation didn't seem to be a word in Jericho's vocabulary; his intensity was part of his genetic makeup, like his hair and eye color.

She found out that Jericho didn't do anything by halves. Something inside her made her want to push him beyond that tightly controlled persona to show what was inside him. Peel away the layers until she found the man beneath.

She walked across the porch and then paused in the spill of white light from a crystal and black wrought-iron lamp. She was almost certain that he was home; a sleek, black Mercedes that pegged him to a T sat in the driveway. All the house windows were dark except for a small amount of light that peeked out of a basement window.

Her mother had taught her never to show up on someone's porch step. But she hadn't wanted to give

Jericho a head's up. It was late, sometime after midnight, and she could have waited to tell him that she should be removed from the case.

But it was more than confessing to him that she wasn't fit to continue with this investigation and certainly shouldn't be put on the witness stand. She'd craved him all afternoon. Her desire gnawed at her.

Kate slid her hand to the tight muscles in the back of her neck. Her mind should be on what she had to do, not on Jericho the man. She was putting herself on the line for Danny because she believed in his innocence. It was in direct conflict with her job. He had to know that she was compromised and not objective at all.

Expelling a slow breath, Kate raised a shaking hand and lifted the ornate knocker and let it fall.

Minutes later the hall light snapped on, flashing through the three panes of glass at the top of the heavy oak door, illuminating the porch in bright light. The dead bolt above the doorknob disengaged with an abrupt snick, then the door swung open.

Kate found herself facing a half-naked, lethal Jericho in tight gray shorts and a white sleeveless T-shirt. A fine sheen misted his body, his hair wet and slicked back off his face.

He certainly was…big, she thought inanely, feeling suffocated by his closeness. He was taller than her, but she had no idea that the impeccably tailored suit had covered this.

His shoulders were so broad they blocked her view of the room. His arms bulged with muscles, as did his chest, which the damp T-shirt clung to revealingly. The power was echoed in the long ropes of muscles in his legs and calves. She fidgeted in spite of herself. Something about all his masculinity intimidated her. Until she looked into his eyes and saw that intensity trained on her. He was going to change her. She knew that, but how and when made her edgy and nervous. It was a change she craved yet feared. She knew who she was, but had always dreamed about who she could be if only…

"Kate? Is something wrong?"

"Yes."

He moved out of the way so that she could step into the foyer. The rug beneath her feet was Oriental and cost a fortune. There was a small occasional table made out of a rich mahogany wood with a mirror over it in the foyer. She caught a glimpse of herself in its polished surface. She looked tired, bone-tired. Her hair was a mess.

She grabbed at her hair, trying to smooth it into place.

"What's wrong, Kate?" His eyes followed her fingers as they worked through her hair.

"I asked Stephen Castle to represent Danny."

His eyes flew to her face. "You *what?*"

"He's doing it *pro bono* but the bottom line is I still asked him. He's doing it as a favor to me."

Jericho closed his eyes and ran his hands through his damp hair. "Come in," he said brusquely. "We can talk in the living room."

Fatigue weighted her as she followed him down the long carpeted hallway past the dining room with its hardwood floor, another more luxurious Oriental rug and thick dark furnishings.

When they stepped into the spacious living room, she took the measure of the beautiful room from the couch and chairs upholstered in a cream-and-red fabric, the tapestry pillows that matched the rug spread out over the polished wooden floor to the breathtaking carved fireplace.

He nodded toward the couch. "Have a seat."

"Are you going to stand?"

"Considering I'm all sweaty from working out, yes."

"Then I will too. I want to remain standing when you fire me."

7

"I HAVE NO INTENTION of firing you," he said, bracing his shoulder against the burnished wood mantel over the fireplace. His gaze went to the books in the nearby built-in shelves.

Taking a deep breath, she settled onto an armchair that sat at an angle to the sofa. "You don't?"

Jericho raised one dark eyebrow, his eyes as emphatic as his voice. "No. No way, not over this."

"How can you be sure that I won't hold something back in court?"

He pushed away from the mantel and took a few steps toward her. "Kate that would never happen. Never," he emphasized.

The tension deflated out of her like a hot air balloon losing altitude. She had no idea that her job had meant so much to her or that Jericho's opinion mattered just as much. "Are you saying that you trust me to do the right thing?"

"Without question."

She couldn't seem to form words at his unequivocal answer. Her parents had revered her. Anything she'd done had awed them. Faculty had praised her. Co-workers held her in great esteem. But the knowledge that Jericho trusted her so implicitly had sudden emotion clogging her throat. It was a defining moment in her life to know that this man found her not only worthy, but considered her beyond reproach.

His eyes softened and the look tugged at her heart. It would take so little effort on his part to make her fall in love with him. Maybe she was already halfway there.

"I think your loyalty is misplaced in this instance, but I admire it tremendously, Kate. Danny's lucky to have such a friend as you."

She finally found her voice. "So, you have no problem with me being on this case."

He took a few more steps and walked over to a bar. Picking up a pitcher of ice water, he poured a glass. Walking over to her, he offered her the water.

She took the glass out of his hand, electricity snapping against her fingers as they brushed his skin.

He went back to the bar and poured another glass. He downed it in three quick swallows and poured another. "If it was up to me, I'd say yes, continue, but the D.A. wants to move forward. He thinks you'd be wasting your time chasing ghosts. He believes that there was no one else in that apartment.

He wants me to go with the evidence that I have that Danny killed her. I argued with him, but it did no good.''

"Obviously you didn't argue hard enough.''

"I think you want to find evidence that someone else was in the apartment, but I think you'll come up empty. You'll have to accept the fact that Danny killed her.''

Sparring with him was something that she knew how to do. Using her mind was second nature to her. It only became hard when she was asked to give more than she could emotionally. Feelings were so unpredictable and had no rhyme or reason. "I don't think so. I'll prove it to you, Jericho, and to the D.A.''

He took another long swallow of the water. "You'll have to do it on your own time and make sure the D.A. doesn't find out.''

"You'd cover for me?''

"Kate, you've been a criminalist for a long time. I believe in turning over every stone to make sure nothing else crawls out. I don't like to be surprised in court. Roth will have us both by the short hairs if he finds out, so be careful and discreet.''

"Okay, that's fine. I don't mind using my free time to prove that Danny's innocent. But I think you should be prepared to postpone the trial.''

"Why is that?''

"I think a competency hearing is in order. Danny has about a seventh grade understanding. He couldn't possibly understand court proceedings."

Jericho finished his water off and set the glass down on the edge of the mantel. "The D.A. has already gotten the judge to waive a competency hearing. He'll be arraigned tomorrow as scheduled and the trial will go forward."

"You agree with the D.A.?" Kate snapped.

"Not entirely, but I don't see any merit in dragging Danny to a competency hearing. He knows right from wrong. That much I gathered when I talked to him."

She stared at him long and hard, her chest heaving with temper, her jaw set so rigid her teeth hurt. She knew that his hands weren't tied. He could order a competency hearing if he wanted to, but he was Roth's fair-haired boy, running for D.A. with his blessing. She nodded. "I see. Now that Roth has endorsed you, you don't want to step on his toes. I'm sorry I disturbed your workout. I'm sure you'll want to get back to it."

"Wait just a damn minute. My decision has nothing to do with my political aspirations."

"Oh, convince me."

"I think Danny's lying because he's scared. He knows the difference between right and wrong, Kate. A competency hearing would cost the taxpayers. It's part of my job to make sure that their money is well spent. I don't think it would be in this case.''

''Danny's not lying.''

''How do you refute the candlestick evidence?''

''Okay, he's lying about that. I'll concede that, but he says he didn't kill Mrs. LePlante.''

''How do you know that?''

''I asked him.''

''Do you think he would tell you the truth?''

''Yes.''

''I don't know, Kate. He knows how you feel about him. He knows you have a place of power, one that could help him. I don't think he's as handicapped as he lets on.''

''Why do you say that?''

''He asked me pretty pointed questions abut the trial. I think he can participate in his own defense.''

''He's got a good defense attorney now. In fact, I think that Stephen Castle is one of the few who has defeated you in the past.''

''He's good, but this time he doesn't have much with which to defend his client. The forensic evidence is overwhelming.''

''It is. I'll give you that. I should go, and let you finish your workout before it gets too late.''

''There's still something I want to discuss with you.'' He stepped forward. ''Are you still mad at me about last night, Katie?''

"No. I wasn't mad at you last night, just feeling cornered."

"Is that what I do to you? Make you feel cornered. Not very flattering."

"I guess not. But I don't want to be pushed into something I'm not ready for."

"We've been playing games now for a while. I'd say it was time for action. If I remember correctly, you threw down the gauntlet."

"And so did you."

"I told you what my reasons were for not pursuing something with you. You didn't tell me yours."

"What? For not pursuing you? How could I do that when every time I came into your presence, you didn't even flutter an eyelash? I figured you weren't interested."

"That's lame, Kate. You are like a pit bull in the lab. I've never seen a more organized woman, so what was it about me that you were afraid to find out?"

"I wasn't afraid."

"Was it that I wouldn't be interested or that I would?"

"Just because you have no doubts about my loyalty and my intelligence doesn't mean you know me."

"I think I do know you. You value the intellectual

world over the physical. You like to classify and categorize. It helps you continue to view life as a mental challenge. But life isn't a spectator sport. It needs to be experienced, Kate. It needs to be embraced.''

"I embrace life. I do everything I can to fulfill my dreams.''

"Do you? From what I can see, you're rigid, repressed and a perfectionist.''

Stung, she faced him. Her chin lifted a notch. She would never let on how much that hurt. ''Well, thank you very much for your assessment of my boring personality. I'm thankful that I have you to point out my flaws.''

She walked past him. The scent of his body reached out and tugged at her, but she ignored it. She ignored the tingling in her nerve endings, ignored the fact that Jericho seemed to be able to reach right down into her psyche and pinpoint her personality as if he was some kind of shrink. She should know better than to try to pull one over on him.

She could do it to other men, but Jericho saw right through her as if she were transparent.

She would have to admit that they had some kind of bond. All the years she'd worked for him had he been watching her, studying her to get an idea of what kind of woman she was. It seemed that he was as intrigued by her mind as he was by her body.

Her arousal hit her like a ton of bricks. The thought that he wanted to explore not only her body but also her mind made her shake inside.

It shook the foundations of her belief of him as a lone wolf prosecutor who cared nothing at all about people. He only wanted to win. But had she been blinded by her own stereotypes of rich men? Men of power who used it to further their own gains?

"Everyone has flaws, Katie. That's what makes them unique. I can be a self-righteous, relentless and merciless bastard when I'm in the courtroom. No one. *No one* is going to escape justice if I have anything to say about it. I'm fanatical about it."

"What do you want from me?"

"I just want to know the woman who put on that red dress and came strutting into the courtroom. I see a side of you that you don't. I know there's heat in you, passion. Wake up, Kate. Let me see you."

"I don't know what you're talking about."

"I think you do. You don't want to admit it to me or to yourself. But I want her, that woman you keep repressed. Oh yes, I want her."

Something inside her snapped. His seductive tone, his hard, accessible body and the way he goaded her made her want to shock him, to give him something to remember. Show him that she wasn't afraid of her own sexuality.

"You want to see her, Jericho?" she asked as she

turned toward him. The material of her skirt brushed against her thighs, sending sensuous tremors all over her body.

A small, rational corner of her brain told her she was taunting a tiger, but she didn't listen. Something inside her was pushing her to recklessness. She didn't understand it, wasn't sure she *wanted* to understand it, but she couldn't seem to stop.

She set her keys on the small table by the door to the hallway and leaned her back into the wall. And the woman she wanted to be was finally set free from her restraints.

She sent the palms of her hands over the silky material covering her hips and down her thighs until she reached the hem of the skirt.

His eyes trailed fire down her body as he followed her hands.

She lifted the hem, rotating her hips against the wall, pulling the material up until she could reach her sex with her hand. Pushing the skimpy bit of thong aside, she slid her fingers into the wet, welcome heat of her body.

"Do you want to know what I fantasize about, Jericho?"

His nostrils flared. "Tell me, Katie. I'm dying to know," he said with an edge to his voice. His eyes watched her hand, every pleasurable nuance on her face as if he could absorb every sensation she felt.

He had eyes that were like a deep, tempting whirl-pool, captivating enough to suck her across the threshold into another dimension, a dark, dangerous dimension.

His thoughts were there in his eyes, exposed, jagged and distinct. His excitement so heavy and thrilling, it left her skin tingling.

"I think about how it would be with you." She slid up her shirt, until her lacy bra was exposed. She cupped her breasts until her cleavage showed. Then she released the clasp of her bra by slowly unsnapping the front and peeling the material away from her breasts.

As he stared at her, his eyes darkened; his gaze on her flesh burned her skin.

Her voice came out hushed and breathless. "I imagine you behind me, your hands sliding over my belly, then cradling my breasts in your hard, hot hands, caressing their softness. I imagine your lips against my throat, your breath warm against my skin, the rasp of your stubble as you kiss my neck and shoulder. I want you to use your tongue and lick the tangy sweetness between my breasts."

Jericho made a growl of appreciative pleasure low in his throat. He made no move toward her, as if he knew she needed to do this, craved it as much as she did. Her awakening.

"I can almost feel the heat and sucking wetness

of your mouth as you kiss and lick me, your tongue swirling and tasting. Your hot mouth fastens over my nipple, making me gasp, hardening the tips and making them throb with the rhythm of my heart. I wonder how you'll take me, finally when we join. Calm and dreamy, or hard and fast. I wonder what kinds of things you could do with that beautiful, clever mouth.''

Her hand slid between her thighs, her words getting bolder the more she aroused herself. ''I see you sink to your knees in supplication, kissing my stomach, pressing your face to my soft curls. Your hot breath causes my hips to surge forward in need, wanting the press of your mouth against that delicious ache between my legs.''

She touched herself, following the path that Jericho's hands would travel if they were on her body. His hands clasped into fists as if he fought his own overwhelming desire. ''You would use those big hands to part my slick folds,'' she gasped, moaning, ''while you tease my stiff, engorged clitoris with your tongue.''

The words coming out of her mouth shocked her as much as she was shocking Jericho. They were urgent and hungry and explicitly detailed. Her mind was racing now and she strove to keep up with each graphic thought.

The hot need in his eyes was almost unbearably

intense. The sense of his resolve weakening made her need pulse in her body, heavy and delicious.

She was overcome by the restless ache between her thighs. With fierce, moaning impatience, she pressed back against the wall, eagerly sliding her sensitized skin against the silky skirt.

Her legs fell open and her fingers slid eagerly into the dampness between her legs. A flurry of sensual images swirled in a tumult behind her eyes. The image of him pushing her legs apart, pressing his face against her sex, his hot mouth closing over her clitoris, sucking with slow, gentle skill, sent sensations twisting through her as she imagined the thrust of his tongue deep into the burning, shuddering heart of her.

She imagined him lifting her against the hard wall, felt the heat, the press of his hard, powerful body. Then glorious contact as he thrust into her with one frenzied stroke, and then staggering pleasure as he pumped his muscled hips against her. She would wrap her arms around him for balance, as an anchor, clutching him tight as he thrust deeper and harder, his powerful arms supporting her, his eyes gazing into hers, seeing her soul revealed, luminescent, fully his.

That pushed her over the top. She arched against the wall with a sharp cry and came. Her body shaking with a continuous shuddering surge of carnal gratification, more forceful than any orgasm she had ever experienced.

She slid against the wall as bright sparks of fire ignited and extinguished, leaving her utterly satisfied, and satiated.

When she opened her eyes, Jericho was no longer on his feet. He was kneeling on the floor, panting; sweat trickled down his temples, over his dark stubble, down his elegant throat.

She'd brought him to his knees. It drove her crazy, tearing down her image of herself, releasing something deeper and fiercer, something heightened and exalted and savagely feminine.

And it frightened her more than anything else ever had.

He looked up at her, his eyes burning, paying homage to her in her wickedness. Softly, his voice ringing with power, he said, ''Come here.''

Adrenaline surged into her body and she dropped her skirt and pushed away from the wall. Snatching up her keys, she turned and ran down the hall.

''Kate!'' Jericho's voice echoed in the hallway and for a moment, the torture, the need in his voice almost stopped her. She was sinking in too deep. *Too deep.* She had to get away. To *hell* with proving herself to anyone. She *needed* to forge her boundaries. She needed to protect herself.

She needed to *run*.

She pulled open the front door and flew down the stairs. Her hands shook so badly she fumbled with the keys. She chanced a glance at Jericho's open door and when he materialized there, she panicked. Shoving the key in, she pulled the door open and jumped inside, jamming the key into the ignition. He was coming down the stairs when she put the car into drive and sped off.

He would follow her. She knew that he wasn't going to allow her to get away from him. So she couldn't go home. She couldn't go to either Lana or Sienna. He would find her there. She didn't know how, but he would.

Paige would be safe. He wouldn't think to look for her there. She would be able to gather her composure and to squash these intense feelings roiling around in her.

How could she have been so bold, so wicked? How could she have let herself go like that in front of him? Those weren't difficult questions. She wanted to. She wanted him to look at her like that. She wanted him to suffer, to want her, to need to touch her. She wanted to bring him to his knees. And she had.

It felt so good, so very good. A man like Jericho wouldn't succumb easily. It had taken everything she'd had to entice him.

Her cell phone rang but she ignored it. She didn't

know what to say to him. She had enjoyed him watching her while she pleasured herself. It wasn't like her to be so free, to abandon all propriety.

Or was it?

Had this wanton woman always existed in her, waiting for the right, darkly sensual man to goad her into it? Or had she always been this way and was too afraid to let herself go as she had tonight?

She parked in front of Paige's house and ran up the walk, knocking on the door.

Paige opened the door with sleepy puzzlement, only to have her face change to alarm. "Dear God, Kate. What's the matter?"

"I took your advice," she said softly and burst into tears.

8

JERICHO SWORE VEHEMENTLY as her car disappeared into the night. Turning, he ran back to the house and up to his bedroom, spending precious minutes fighting his pants' pocket for his keys.

He ran back down the stairs and got into his car. He squealed out of his driveway and drove as fast as he could to Kate's house. Once there he parked and bolted out of the car. He banged on her door, but no one answered. Swearing again, he went back to his car.

Inside the vehicle, he rested his head against the steering wheel. Christ, he was still hard and hot, his blood throbbing heavy through his veins. What the hell had happened?

Ha. Don't you know, hotshot? It had finally happened. Kate had come into her own and it had scared her. She was also probably embarrassed as hell that she had gotten herself off in front of him.

He, on the other hand, wanted to howl at the moon. He didn't want her to wallow in her embarrassment tonight. He felt desperate to get to her.

Desperate to tell her how much she turned him on. How much he wanted to slide into her. He could think of nothing else.

Then, after he had sated his body, he wanted to hold her against him, to fall asleep to the rhythm of her heart. He wanted to breathe her fragrance and float in the sheer gift of her presence.

He picked up his cell phone and dialed in the police station. When the voice answered at the end of the line, he said, "This is D.D.A. Jericho St. James. I need the addresses of Sienna Parker and Lana Dempsey."

Two HOURS LATER he was even more frustrated than before. Sienna had been no help, saying that she hadn't even talked to Kate that day. Lana had been ruder. She'd said that if he'd screwed up and hurt Kate, she'd kick his ass.

Now both women were up and worried about Kate, just as he was.

He picked up the phone again and dialed. This time he got Eric Banner's address.

When he banged on Banner's door, the light came on after a few minutes and Eric opened the door, squinting against the harsh outside light.

"What the hell, Jericho?"

"Is Kate here?"

Eric looked utterly confused. "Kate?"

"Banner, just tell me if she's here."

"She's not," he assured, his hands coming up in front of him as if to ward Jericho off. "What the hell happened?"

"It's a long and very private story."

Eric ran his hands through his hair. "Come in. Maybe I can help."

Jericho went into Eric's neat house and sat on his comfortable sofa.

Eric brought out a whiskey bottle and two glasses.

"What is that for?"

"I'm helping. If Kate doesn't want to be found, the only thing you can do is drown your sorrows in a bottle."

Jericho picked up the bottle, pulled off the top and took a long swig.

"Damn, man. You don't fool around."

Jericho closed his eyes as the alcohol burned a long, hot trail to his stomach. The look of panic on Kate's face twisted like a knife in his gut. He couldn't stand the fact that he would frighten her. He took another hefty slug and Eric grabbed the bottle.

"Whoa, Jericho."

Jericho ran his hands over his face and closed his eyes to gather his composure.

"What happened?"

"Kate and I had…an argument. She left and I'm sorry. I want to tell her so, but I can't find her."

"Do you want my advice?"

"Not particularly."

"I'm going to give it to you, anyway. Kate does things in her own time. She can't be goaded or pushed into anything she doesn't want to do. And when she gets mad. Hoo boy, watch out."

"How come you know so much about her?"

"I don't have any designs on her, St. James, but if you break her heart, I'll have to punch your lights out."

"Thanks for the warning."

"Sure. Now back to Kate. She's really smart."

"I know…"

"I mean really, really smart. I've seen her find evidence that all of us have missed. She's relentless, tough, and never gets discouraged."

"I believe that, Banner."

All the while they talked, Jericho drank. The drunker he got, the more he worried about Kate.

"You know, the last time I got this drunk, I got a tattoo."

"Where?"

"Groin."

"Ouch. Did it hurt?"

"Don't remember a damn thing, but when I woke up in the morning with a mother of a hangover, it hurt like hell. I've got a feeling I'm going to feel the same way when I wake up tomorrow.''

Jericho's eyes drifted shut and his last thought was for Kate.

KATE STARED open-eyed at the beach scene in Paige's spare room. Paige had coddled her and soothed her and given her a room to sleep in for the night.

To keep her mind off Jericho and her performance, Kate turned her thoughts to Danny's case. She went over the crime scene in her mind, bit by bit. She was convinced that someone had surprised Marie LePlante. She believed that the woman had been knocked to the carpet by Danny's blow and he'd left the apartment. She had gone to the bathroom mirror to check her wound and to clean it. That's what most people would do. She'd been staring in the mirror and…he'd been hiding in the shower. Kate was sure of it. Mrs. LePlante had seen him and had whirled away from the sink to confront him. Kate didn't believe that she would have run. Maybe she'd recognized him and it had momentarily paralyzed her? The assailant had jumped out of the shower and grabbed Mrs. LePlante around the neck, shoving her into the full-length mirror. There'd been an indentation in the glass that was the exact size of her head, but there'd also been another one below it. The blood on the sink and the depression in the glass could have come from the assailant shoving her into the mirror. Kate replayed her encounter with Ken Mitchell over in her mind….

He'd had his hands in his pockets. Could he have been hiding his hands to cover small cuts? It occurred to her that he'd told her there were a rash of burglaries in her building. It would make sense that Danny was committing the crimes because he had access to every apartment. But Danny wouldn't do such a thing.

She made a mental note to go see Sienna after Danny's arraignment tomorrow morning.

The thought of Danny's arraignment made her remember that Jericho would be there. Paige had called Sienna and Lana to let them know where Kate was. Sure enough, Jericho had been there.

Kate hadn't been up to talking to them. She'd told Paige that she promised to explain everything tomorrow.

Losing her cool at Jericho's had been nothing but cowardice. She was ashamed of herself for acting like such a fool. She was going to tell him tomorrow as soon as she got the chance.

With that resolution, she closed her eyes and fell asleep.

JERICHO BOLTED UP off the couch for a moment, disoriented. Then he grabbed his head and groaned.

As Eric came out of the kitchen, the aroma of bacon twisted Jericho's stomach.

"I was just about to wake you. Do you have court today?"

"What time is it?"

"Six."

Jericho relaxed back into the cushions. "I don't have to be there until eight."

"Head hurt?"

"Like a bitch."

"There's aspirin in the bathroom and water in the fridge."

"Thanks, Banner."

"Sure. Give Kate some space, she'll come around. She's stubborn."

Jericho groaned when he got to his feet, heading directly to the bathroom, he took care of his insistent bladder, grabbed aspirin and water. In his car, he wanted to go by Kate's apartment to see if she was home, but he realized that Banner was right. He needed to give her space. She'd come around. At least, he hoped that she would.

One hour later he was showered, shaved and dressed in a charcoal suit. He slipped his dove gray tie around the pale gray shirt and had to knot it twice but still couldn't get it right. Damn, the woman had turned him inside out last night. She should have been in his bed this morning, in his shower, in his damn arms right now.

He cursed the tie and pulled it from around his neck. With another curse, he undid the top button of his shirt because he felt as though he was strangling.

He'd do the damn thing when he got to court.

HE WALKED INTO the courthouse and realized that he was running late. He took the stairs up to the courtroom, but stopped outside the doors to put on his tie.

He couldn't get it done, because there wasn't a mirror.

A feminine hand slid over his and his head jerked up to find Kate standing in front of him.

"Here. Let me help you with that."

"Kate," he breathed as she took the two ends of his tie and deftly tied it right. The first time.

"I'm sorry."

Her head jerked up and she smiled softly. "Thanks. You look like hell, by the way."

A grin spread across his face. "Talk to Banner. It's his fault."

The bailiff went to close the courtroom doors and Jericho had no more time to talk to Kate.

The first three arraignments went quickly, and then Danny was brought in. He was dressed in a suit that Stephen must have gotten for him. Already she felt better about asking him to defend Danny. He would do the best job he could.

The judge read Danny his rights. The rights Kate had explained to him the day before.

The judge asked. "How do you plead?"

Danny said, "Not guilty."

"Mr. St. James, bail?"

"The state requests the court set bail at five hundred thousand dollars."

"Objection," Stephen said. "Mr. Hamilton is a handyman with a diminished capacity. He is no risk to the community."

"Your Honor, Mr. Hamilton violently strangled a woman to death in her apartment. I'd say his temper is questionable and he'd be a threat to the community," Jericho argued.

"Bail is set at five hundred thousand dollars."

The judge scheduled a preliminary hearing for one week later, any pretrial motions for four weeks later, a pretrial conference for six weeks later and trial for seven weeks later. Then he banged his gavel and said, "Next case."

The schedule would give Kate time to analyze the blood and the fibers found at the crime scene and that exculpatory evidence would give Stephen ammunition to blow holes in Jericho's case.

Kate looked at her watch. She really wanted to talk to him, but she wasn't sure how long he would be.

She rose and caught Stephen Castle's eye. He looked as though he wanted to talk to her.

He followed her out of the courtroom and she cast one more look over her shoulder. Jericho was watching her with the same longing on his face. She smiled at him and left the courtroom.

She spent an hour with Stephen going over all the evidence. He asked numerous questions and got permission from her to visit the crime scene.

"So, I guess that the look you threw Jericho St. James would make it a moot point for me to ask you out to dinner?"

She smiled. "Yes, I'm afraid so, but I appreciate the invite."

"You look good, Kate. St. James was always a lucky bastard."

After he left, Kate went over to Jericho's office. She went up to Sandy and said, "Is Jericho in?"

Sandy shook her head. "Sorry, he's in court until five."

"Thanks." Thwarted from talking to Jericho, Kate headed over to the precinct to talk to Sienna about the rash of burglaries.

The minute Sienna saw her, she rose from her desk. "Are you all right?"

"I'm fine. It was just a case of cold feet."

"Have you talked to Jericho yet?"

"Briefly, but he had to do arraignments this morning and is in court all afternoon."

"What happened?"

"We had this contest going about who could lose their cool first. He challenged me and I…got myself off in front of him."

"You what? Ohmigod Kate!"

"Afterward I got scared."

"Why?"

"I should have taken my cue from you and Lana. This isn't as simple as it seems on the surface. I have feelings for him."

"Have you told him?"

"No, not yet, but I will. I wanted to ask you about the fact that my building has been burglarized. Did you know about that?"

"No, but I can find out for you."

After a few moments on the phone, Sienna hung up. "Burglary said they had no leads, guy wore gloves, stole small things, never cash. It was always something sentimental to the victim."

"Couldn't they trace the stuff after it was fenced."

"Never fenced."

"So, no profit?"

"No. Burglary's not sure why. They did say that all the apartments showed no signs of forced entry."

"Someone had a key?"

"Looks that way. They checked out Daniel Hamilton, who's the super, but couldn't pin anything on him. They even watched him for a week. He never went into an apartment unless he was fixing something. He was a dead end."

"Who would have duplicate keys?"

"The owner?"

"Bingo."

"They checked out anybody who had access to keys, Kate. They were all clean."

"Yeah, well, we'll see about that."

THE MITCHELL CORPORATE offices were located in the heart of the city in the prestigious and posh Cooper Building.

She walked up to the receptionist's station and asked for the senior Mr. Mitchell's office. Stepping into the elevator, she rode to the twenty-seventh floor and walked into his office.

His secretary looked up at Kate over her half glasses, like a librarian who's sure she's found the perfect candidate to be loud in the library.

"May I help you?"

"I'd like to see Mr. Mitchell."

"Do you have an appointment?"

"No, but I think he'll see me."

"Why is that, miss?"

"It's about the murder that took place in his downtown building. The one I live in."

"Just a moment." She picked up the phone and buzzed his office.

Moments later he came out of his office. "Miss Quinn. What a surprise to find out it's you who wants to see me."

"I have a few questions for you, if you have a few minutes."

"Certainly."

Kate was ushered into his office and she sat in one of the posh chairs.

"What can I do for you?"

"I want to know who has control of the master keys for our apartments?"

"Why, I do, of course."

"Where are they kept?"

"In my safe here in the corporate offices."

"Who has access to that safe?"

"Just me."

"Your son doesn't have the combination?"

"Ken? What does this have to do with Ken?"

"I'm just asking the question, Mr. Mitchell."

"Is this about the burglaries?"

"As a matter of fact, it is."

"I thought you were a forensic specialist. Why would you have any interest in burglaries?"

"I do live in the building. One woman was mur-

dered there and three apartments have been burglarized.''

''But you're not here because of that. You're here
for that Hamilton fellow. The one arrested for the
murder of my tenant.''

''I think Danny's innocent.''

Mr. Mitchell's face got red. ''Balderdash. He's as
guilty as the police believe he is. I'll see him behind
bars for putting a stain on my reputation as an apartment owner. I should have never listened to Ken
when he wanted to hire the man. This interview is
over.''

Kate walked out of Mitchell's office and ran right
into Ken.

''Ms. Quinn. What brings you to my father's office?''

She looked down at Ken's hands, but they were
in his pockets.

She brushed past him and exited the building. She
was convinced that Ken was in Mrs. LePlante's
apartment. The why she didn't know for sure, but
she was going to prove that he was there.

She hailed a cab. There was one more stop she
had to make before she went home.

WHEN KATE GOT TO the hallway of her building,
Jericho was there, pacing. When he stepped out of
the shadow into the silvery light, he looked beat.

She had no idea what he had been doing all day, but although she knew he'd had a rough night and a busy day, he still looked...driven. It didn't matter to her how he looked. It had been inevitable from the beginning. It was time to stop playing games. He was so handsome in his black silk T-shirt that molded against the contours of his chest and the tight, faded jeans took his danger quotient up a notch. The devil in blue jeans. His hair was mussed, as if he'd been running his hands through it for hours. It was such a sharp contrast to the perfectly coiffed, impeccably dressed, fully-in-control prosecutor that she stopped dead in the hall to take it all in.

She took in the view of all that prowling male energy. The man must exude it out of his pores. His charisma was a tangible thing. His eyes cleared when he saw her.

Inside she was in turmoil, but she acted carefully nonchalant when she walked toward him.

"What the hell do you think you're doing?"

It wasn't what she'd expected him to say and she immediately bristled at his growling tone. "I'm coming home from work and having to deal with a jerk."

"Huh."

"That would be you. The jerk."

"I'm sorry. I got a call from the D.A. and he was

mad as hell about one of his employees harassing one of his biggest campaign contributors. What were you thinking?''

''I'm thinking that Ken Mitchell killed Mrs. LePlante and framed Danny for it.'' She shoved her key into the lock and opened the door.

He pushed his way inside and slammed the door behind him. She almost didn't know this out-of-control, frantic man.

''It's not your job to investigate leads. That's for the police.''

''I don't give a damn, Jericho. I'm not going to let Danny go to jail! If that ruins your precious campaign contributor's day, that's too damn bad!''

''I don't give a damn about him. You can harass his whole damn family. I…need you. I'm desperate for you.'' He clasped her around the waist and sank to his knees, still clutching her waist.

She went limp with shock. Jericho was begging her. Finally, he was begging her. She could only feel sorry she'd made him wait when all she'd wanted to do from the moment she'd laid eyes on him was to slide into his arms, into a maelstrom of sensations and emotions.

She stared down into his hot, dark eyes; a hot, trembling sensation was spreading throughout her body. Her fingers threaded through his soft brown hair. His chin was pressed against her navel, and he gripped her hips, the intense warmth of his big hands sinking through the fabric.

Her throat was vibrating, her whole body was vibrating, as if she were about to shake apart.

"Please," she whispered. She reached down and grabbed his shoulders. "Jericho, I can't bear it."

He leaned his head back and closed his eyes, shaking his head in helpless frustration. "Please believe me, I really don't want to wreck this."

The baffled hurt in his voice pained her. "You didn't," she blurted out. "You haven't. But I can't just let myself go like you want me to. Or at least…I shouldn't."

"You did a pretty good job of that at my house last night. I've thought of nothing else. You were…amazing. I've been hard on and off all day thinking about every breathless moment," he murmured, his voice low and textured like raw silk—rough and smooth at once, beckoning a woman to reach out and touch him, tempting her, luring her closer.

He pressed his nose against her stomach and breathed deeply. "Last night, the way you felt. It scared you."

"Down to my toes. I've never felt so turned on, so lustful."

"Ever?"

"It's you Jericho. I want to turn myself on for

you.'' Since he refused to stand she slid to her knees. ''The way you looked at me. The way you wanted me. I've craved that for years before I ever knew you. It was you I wanted.''

''Damn,'' he breathed. ''I'm wondering how we waited so long.''

''I don't know.''

''Fear? Stupid inner rules. Who knows? It ends now, Kate.''

''Yes, please. I can't wait for you any longer.'' She leaned forward and pressed her lips to his rough face. The temptation to let herself go tugged harder on her.

As his lips found her throat and he began to kiss her with teasing little taste-testing kisses, the temptation grew stronger.

''Jericho, you have the most beautiful—'' she broke off at the breathless sound of her voice ''—mouth.''

He chuckled wickedly against her neck, sliding a hand up and down her upper arms, his thumb brushing seductively against the side of her breast. ''Wait until I show you what I can do with it.''

9

A JOLT OF PURE LONGING shuddered through her and her hands went into his hair. The strands were so soft. She twisted in his grasp and clasped his hand, guiding him to her breast. She had ignored her physical needs for so long, she had forgotten what it was to want a man.

No, that wasn't quite right. The realization flashed through the haze of her desire. She had *never* known what it was to want a man. Not the way she wanted Jericho. She had grown up suppressing her sexuality, avoiding the unknown quicksand of desire and want, using her mind to forge ahead.

She'd been wrong. As Jericho placed tantalizing kisses down her slender throat to the tender curve of her shoulder, desire ignited inside her like tinder to an out-of-control flame. It excited her, drew her even as it frightened her.

''Show me,'' she pleaded, her muscles melting with the warmth of desire.

''It'll be my pleasure,'' he murmured, kissing his way back up her neck to her ear. He traced the tip of his tongue around the rim of the delicate shell, took the lobe between his lips and sucked gently.

"I burn for you, Kate." To prove his point, he caught her hand and pressed it to the front of his jeans, thrusting her palm against his erection, holding her there while he brushed kisses along her jaw to the corner of her mouth and explored her lips skillfully with the tip of his tongue. "I want you," he whispered seductively.

Kate shivered like a woman in the grasp of a raging fever, hot then cold, on the verge of incoherence. Logic evaporated in the wake of Jericho's sensual assault. He covered her hand with his and molded her fingers over the proof of his words. He was hard and throbbing and an answering pulse pounded in the pit of her belly. She stole a breath and felt her knees wobble beneath her.

"I don't usually have casual sex."

His expression grew serious, intense, as he stared down at her and a tremor went through her. This Jericho looked like a dominant male, a predator, capable of anything.

"There's nothing casual about this." He lifted his hand and cupped her cheek, the fire in his eyes flaring. "About us."

Then he lowered his head and kissed her, insistently, demanding and provoking. His lips, firm and smooth and oh, so clever, moved against hers, rubbed over hers, seduced hers into her own ravenous response. He inched a step closer. Raising his other hand and sliding his fingers back into her silky hair, he tugged her head back for a better angle.

"Yes, Kate," he murmured. "I want it all. Give it to me. Kiss me harder," he commanded on a phantom breath. "Take me, taste me."

Jericho's mouth moved relentlessly over hers, claiming, beguiling, seducing, giving so much pleasure her head swam.

With a deep groan, she obeyed his command, working her lips frantically against his. Her fingers curled into the fabric of his shirt, pressing up against the steely muscles of his chest.

Jericho stood abruptly and brought her with him. He groaned at her surrender and deepened the kiss. With firm, sensuous strokes, he eased his tongue into her mouth, probing deeply, brazenly. She responded to him with an enthusiastic maneuver of her own, her tongue tracing his lower lip, dipping inside his mouth.

He sucked at her gently, and need overwhelmed her like a vise as she trembled strongly against him.

Unable to wait any longer to feel his skin against hers, she boldly swept her hands down to his waist and the hem of his shirt. Eagerly, she pulled his shirt over his head and tossed it aside. Heat poured through her, molten, liquid heat, searing her veins, pooling in her groin. He gasped when her hands glided back up his hard, hot chest.

Kate swept her hands over the smooth, solid muscles and contours of his body, exploring his strength. She couldn't get enough of touching him, wanted to press into him and feel that power and heat against the length of her and absorb it through her skin. When his hands settled on her waist and he touched the hem of her top, Kate groaned at the feel of his hands against the bare skin of her waist. With one sweep, he pulled it over her head and away from them. The removal of her bra was a whisper of silk and lace.

She stepped closer to him, her breasts jutting out, aching for contact. What was left of her breath evaporated as her breasts flattened against him, her nipples burning and aching at the contact.

Jericho growled low in his throat as he kissed her. He trailed his fingertips down the indentation of her spine, stroking every inch of her skin, every hollow. Dragging her against him, he lifted her hips to his. The hard ridge of his arousal broadcast loud and clear how badly, how urgently, he wanted her. She wrapped her arms around him, her breasts sliding against the hard wall of his chest. She kissed his throat, his shoulder. Her tongue dipped into the spot at the base of his throat and desire surged through her.

His fingers fumbled with the button and zipper at the back of her skirt. Kate sent her hands back there to cover his, aiding him, her heart contracting at the way his hands trembled. With frantic hands, he sent the tailored skirt down around her ankles. His fingers played with the waistband of her blue lace panties, his fingers like licks of flame against her skin.

At last she was naked in his arms. His eyes flashed heat in the quiet room as he drank in the sight of her with starving eyes.

"Exquisite," he whispered. He pulled her tight against him. His mouth found hers again and he kissed her with a hunger that spoke volumes.

Kate moaned, reveling in the sheer texture of his mouth, the heady scent of a powerfully aroused male. She was beyond need as Jericho bent her back over his hard, muscled forearm. This was what Paige had been talking about, the full, carnal experience of a man and a woman. It made her so acutely aware that she had been doing nothing but merely existing. This was life at its essence, at its most intense. It throbbed through her, pulsed within her, made her ache with hunger.

She arched into his touch when his hand closed over her breast. He cupped it gently and gasped as the need for his touch burst inside her. The shattering sensations his fingers evoked as they played over her flesh made her breath shallow and quick. When he slicked both hands down her spine and over her buttocks, kneading, squeezing, she slid her arms around his neck and rose up again on tiptoe against him, offering all that she was. His fingertips traced down the center line, his eyes taking great pleasure in watching her reaction. She gasped at his exploration, his fingers arousing and knowing set off detonations of utter sensual ecstasy, skipped across each nerve ending to coil and vibrate at the base of her spine. Then his hand slipped between their bodies and he speared his fingers into the nest of soft curls that covered her femininity, and fire burst through her, taking her breath. With each slide of his skillful fingers, her hips jerked forward and back uncontrollably.

''That's it,'' he whispered, stroking the silken, moist, ultrasensitive flesh between her thighs. ''Want me. Show me how you'll move when my cock is inside you.''

Slowly he lowered her to the blue cushions of the couch directly behind her, following her down, sprawling over her. She arched her back off the cushion as he found her breasts with his mouth, capturing her nipple between his lips and sucking hard on the aching tip, then stroking her with his tongue. He repeated the process again and again, until she thought she couldn't stand the sweet torment a second longer, then he captured the other straining nipple and feasted on her.

Kate entwined her hands in his dark hair and moved impatiently beneath him, soft, wild sounds of longing thrummed in her throat. She wrapped her legs around his hips, the denim of his jeans rough against the sensitive skin of her inner thighs, the abrasion setting off explosions in her groin. Lifting her hips against his belly, she sought contact with the hardest part of his body, seeking to assuage the vital ache that burned at the crux of her desire.

With his thumb he pushed against her stiff, swollen clit. With a deep moan, Kate opened her legs to his touch, aching for him to fill the hot, tight, silken pocket between her thighs.

He delved into her sheath, sinking deep, then almost retreating from her, widening his fingers as he eased out of her, holding her open for a beat before thrusting deep into her again.

"Oh, Jericho!" she cried, frantic, helpless, on the aching brink of fulfillment.

He raised his head and smiled at her. Her lips, swollen from his kiss, moist and parted, begged for him as another part of her was begging for him.

"You like this," he whispered, stroking deep, then easing slowly out of her, opening her, stretching her.

"Yes," she gasped, lifting her hips, trying to urge him into her again.

"Think how good it'll be when my cock is deep inside you," he coaxed in a silky-smooth voice. "I want to see you come again," he murmured. He kissed her quivering stomach, mouth open, hot, wet tongue dipping into her navel. "Do you want it as bad as I do, Katie?"

"I want you inside me."

"Have you ever taken what you want, Katie? Really taken."

She sucked in a heated breath and writhed in response to the coil of craving that constricted and squeezed within her. She'd never been more ready, never wanted like this. She reared up, pushing on his shoulders, shoving him back against the cushions of her couch with all her strength.

She reached for the button on his jeans, grasping at the zipper tab, desperate to free him.

His body tightened as if in a vise and he moaned softly at her show of force. She fought to get the zipper down over his erection. Just as she did so, his cock appeared as if spring loaded.

At this moment Kate didn't know the meaning of the word patience. She wanted Jericho. Now. She reached for him again as he shoved his jeans down. Sitting up, she pressed fervent kisses to his chest as she closed her fingers around his thick, pulsing shaft.

She had barely gotten her mouth around the head of his erection when he jerked her away. "No," he said hoarsely. "I can't last and I want to be inside you."

She tumbled him back onto the cushions. He slashed a hand across himself to keep her from taking him into her body. Momentarily confused, Kate looked down into his eyes.

They were like chunks of burning wood. "Protection," he whispered hoarsely. She pushed his hand aside and protected him herself before guiding him to her. He squeezed his eyes shut as she eased his tip into her. His chest was heaving. Every muscle quivered with the strain of holding himself back. Then Kate took the decision away from him, surging over him, taking half of him before crying out.

"Jericho! Oh, Jericho!"

"Take me, Kate," he whispered between clenched teeth. She was almost out of her mind with pleasure, wanting nothing more than to bury him deep within her.

Kate moaned, caught between agony and ecstasy, wanting to take all of him, sure it was physically impossible. Fighting for breath, she fell forward, belly to belly, chest to chest. Grabbing at his upper arms for support, biceps hard as rock beneath her fingertips, she said breathlessly, "You're so wonderfully big and deliciously thick."

His eyes flared at her admission, his head pressing hard into the couch, his breath erratic. ''Damn, Kate, you're making me crazy,'' he said on a hard exhale.

Enjoying this wonderful power over him, she eased a little deeper, a little deeper, teasing him beyond his and her limits. He surged up and captured one of her nipples, his hands going to her bottom. She fully expected him to take control and thrust his hips, driving his wonderfully hard cock full-length inside of her. But he held back, the strain showing in the corded muscles of his throat. This teasing process was exquisite torture. His hands cupped her face, dragging her mouth to his as he kissed her frantically, hotly whispered to her, coaxed her, teased her, making her gasp and groan uncontrollably.

''Kate, please ride me. Hard and fast. Take me all—I'm dying,'' he begged, rubbing his mouth against her oversensitive lips.

Kate closed her eyes and slammed her hips down on him, taking him fully into her body. His mouth broke off in mid-kiss, turning his head to the side, moaning deep in his chest. His teeth sank into the side of her neck as he murmured hot, sexy words to her as they moved together. The pleasure built and intensified, swelling inside her until she could barely breathe for the pressure of it.

Jericho's kisses grew more urgent, more carnal,

his thrusts deeper, driving, straining, filling her to bursting. The time for play faded, paled in the face of something hot and intense that enveloped them and threatened to consume them. Something like fear gripped Kate by the throat, and she tightened her hold on him, not sure where this was taking her or what would happen after.

''Don't fight it,'' he whispered urgently, feeling the tension in her. He rubbed his cheek against hers, swept her hair back from her face, stared up into her eyes, open and giving and beautifully, erotically Jericho. ''Don't fight it. Let it happen.''

He slipped a hand between them and touched the tender nerve center of her desire, taking her over the edge. Kate cried out wildly as her climax hit her with the power of an explosion from within. She arched over him, hands slipping on his sweat-slicked chest, her muscles clenching around his erection with a force that made the pleasure go on and on and on.

When Jericho's climax hit him, she wrapped her arms around him and thrust herself, hard to the hilt, giving her a hot rush of fulfillment.

Exhausted, she sank down onto his chest, her muscles trembling and relaxing one group at a time. Her breath sawed in and out of her lungs. Her heart was galloping like a racehorse. Feeling dazed, she raised her head and somehow found the strength to smile.

"Wow," he said.

Now that the heated passion was spent, color flooded her cheeks at the wanton way she had taken him. Unable to meet his eyes, she turned her face away from him.

"Oh, no," he said softly, skimming his fingertips along her jaw. "I can feel your heart beat, sweet Kate. It's wonderful."

"Jericho, about last night…"

"You wanted to shock me?"

"Yes, but that's not what I was going to say."

"What were you going to say?"

"I'm sorry I ran out on you. It was a reaction to my own boldness."

"I come on strong. I know I do. It's always been one of my flaws. When I want something, I tend to go overboard."

"Ambition and desire are not flaws."

"No, not in what they do for you. But when you can't be patient, it could get scary."

"I was scared."

"Of me?"

"Of the passion. It was very overwhelming."

"You looked so beautiful. I couldn't take my eyes off you."

"I'm still afraid."

"Is that why you fought what your body so desperately wanted?"

"Yes."

"Kate, it's a natural thing, sex. Most people don't even think about it."

"Maybe I think too much then because I do think about it. It might have been easy for you, Jericho. Your mother and father probably pushed you forward, made you experience life, even encouraged it."

"Yours didn't?"

"Mine couldn't figure me out. They didn't know who I was. Oh, they loved me very much, but they didn't know what to do with me. They acquiesced to everything without any advice. My parents are uncomplicated, simple people who did the best they could."

"That made you a loner?"

"It made me self-reliant and I like that. Other people give me advice, but I go with what I think."

"What about sex?"

"I don't have much experience there."

"Hmm. You could have fooled me."

"When I touched myself in front of you, it made me feel…"

"Vulnerable?"

"Yes. I guess that's why I got spooked. I realized that if I had to lower my barriers that much, just to show you how bold I was, what would it be like to allow you to touch me, slide into my body.''

"But you wanted that. I could see it on your face.''

"I did and it made me angry when you said I was repressed.''

"Why?''

"Because I knew it was true and I wanted to prove you wrong.''

"You want to explore me, Kate? Explore away. If your scientist mind wants to push me to my limits and see what happens, hell, I'm there.''

"You push me harder than anyone I've ever met.''

"But it makes you hot when I push,'' he pointed out. "I can sense it. Pushing you is the only way to get you there. By pushing you to that pinnacle, you can soar, Kate, just the way you want to. Let all of your inhibitions go.''

It was hard to structure what she wanted to say with his eyes deep and penetrating, breaking her concentration. She closed her eyes to gain her composure. "The ones I repress.''

"Yes.''

"But I've never been aggressive.''

"I've heard differently. When you're pressed to the wall, you snarl like a she-wolf. So don't give me that crap.''

She blinked at him. No one had ever talked to her like this. Maybe she'd been too pampered and indulged. She liked that he didn't pull his words to save her embarrassment, but to make her think harder.

"Don't give me that innocent look. You can't hide from me. I can see right into you."

"I know you can. It makes me crazy the way your eyes seem to take in everything." Intrigued, the fear she felt at revealing herself to him paled in comparison to her need to know, in words, what he saw. "Tell me what you see."

"Something volatile. Hot, volcanic and primal. It draws me mercilessly. Makes me insane and restless."

The sound of that restless quality to his voice made her edgy. She moved against him to feel the texture of his skin sliding over hers. She wanted to crawl inside him. "How hard are you going to push?"

"Hard," he said, his lips playing over her cheekbone. "I want to see how far you'll go."

"You want me to surrender. It goes both ways. I need a compromise."

"What compromise?"

"You tell me why you really pretended not to want me for...how long?"

"Since the moment I met you. I was afraid that I couldn't let go."

"You don't have to. Not yet."

"No. Not yet."

He took her hand and guided it to his new erection. "Being with you turns me on so much that I can't think. I can't breathe. I just want to be inside you."

"Jericho," she said softly as she caressed his face, her hands sliding down the strong column of his throat, over the heavy pectoral muscles, to his waist. She pushed at his shoulders until he was beneath her.

As she accepted him into her body, she tried not to want more, but she did. She wanted to talk to him, to see the fire in his eyes when he spoke about his work, his dedication to it. She wanted so much more than his body, but unfortunately, that's all she'd bargained for. That and a souvenir.

10

IT WAS STILL DARK when Kate woke. The sound of soft piano music came from the living room.

She got out of bed. It had taken them time, but they'd finally moved to her room. She tripped over her jeans and a metallic clinking made her bend down. She reached into the pocket and pulled out his cuff links.

She'd totally forgotten about them. She slipped them into the pocket of her silky robe and went into the living room.

He was at the piano, his fingers moving slowly, caressing the keys. His chest was bare, the faded denim jeans molding to his hips and long legs. His bare feet pressed the pedals and caused a little quiver to shudder through her. His head was tipped back, his eyes closed and from his fingers flowed the whispered strains of a haunting, beautiful sound.

She watched as he played, her eyes centering on his long-fingered hands, so big and competent.

The baby grand had been a gift to herself. It had to be hauled up to her apartment, a major undertaking, but she'd wanted the gleaming instrument. It symbolized beauty and artistry. Things that were lacking in the stark world of forensic science. It was her job and she did it well, enjoying the sheer mind power it took to unlock the mysteries of crime. But there was another side to her.

The side of grace and beauty. The hunger to explore and develop something that had never been encouraged as she'd grown. Teachers had loved her mind and had pooh-poohed her penchant for music. But Kate had never let it go. Hence, the baby grand and the music sitting on it.

It touched something inside her to see Jericho moving the white keys and bringing forth from the instrument sheer beauty, something she could only strive to do.

Kate tucked her hands into the pockets of her robe, fingering the cuff links with her right hand, the metal warming to her touch.

Jericho made no move to acknowledge her presence, even when she sat beside him on the piano bench. He went on playing like a man in a trance, his long fingers stroking the keys with the care of a lover. The song rose and fell, melodies twining around one another, wrapping around Kate and taking her into another world, a world of stark poignancy and thundering emotion. Every note swelled with longing. A lingering, hushed beauty filled the silences in between.

This was what hid behind the other Jericho, the man with the formidable determined ambition and the aura of danger—loneliness, beauty, artistry. The realization struck a chord deep within her, and she closed her eyes against the surprise. How many other layers were there? How many Jerichos? Which one was at the core of the man? Which one held his heart?

She closed her mind to the questions and laid her head against his shoulder, too overwhelmed by feelings to think. Always a very bad sign for her. She had held herself in tight check for a long, long time against emotions that had tried to surface. But now, with no defenses against him, she was unable to fight. The feelings rushed up through her chest to her throat and clogged there in a hard lump. The tears came sliding down her face, spiking her lashes and dampening her cheeks.

Jericho's hands slowed on the keyboard as the piece softened to its close. His fingers crept down to touch the final note, a low minor chord that vibrated and hung in the air like the echo of a voice from the dark past.

''That was beautiful.''

''Do you cry at the opera, too?''

''I don't know. I haven't been.''

"We'll have to remedy that."

"You play so well."

"My mother insisted."

Even though he settled his fingers on the piano keys once again and started to play something slow and bluesy, she caught the caustic note in his voice. Slowly she straightened away from him, her gaze sharp and direct. "What do you mean?"

He continued to play until Kate cupped his chin and turned him toward her. He smiled without humor. "Only that it was the best education for me and that included music. I don't have anything against my mother. She's a delightful woman. It's the system that bothers me."

"The injustice of it?"

He turned back to the keys. "You are very perceptive, Kate. Do you want to know the boring details of why I became a prosecutor? What formulated my insatiable pursuit of justice?"

"Yes. If you want to tell me, and I won't find anything about you boring at all."

"A lot of people would call me cold, calculating and ruthless." He held up his hand. "Don't deny it, Kate. I believe you've pointed that out to me just recently when I blocked your attempt at a competency hearing for Mr. Hamilton."

"Everyone has their flaws, Jericho."

"Touché, Kate. You were right. My education

was carefully thought out and faultlessly applied. I saw inequities even at the upstanding school where I was a student.''

''That's the way of society. The haves and have-nots.''

''That's true. But our society is also based on independent ingenuity and a have-not can become a have with a good old-fashioned work ethic.''

''There was such a person in your school?''

''There was. Andrew Matheson.''

''The pianist?''

''One and the same. You see, Andrew's parents could barely afford to send him to the posh school, but somehow they did it. There was a scholarship, a really fat one. Money, I didn't need, but I was entered in the contest and I came in first.''

''Let me guess. Andrew was better than you.''

''Ten times. Music wasn't something that I intended to pursue. It was something I enjoyed, more of a hobby.''

''But even if you had decided to pursue music, you would have turned down the scholarship.''

He turned to look at her, his dark eyes glittering in the darkness. ''That you said that makes me so glad that I try every day to be a better man.''

''You did turn it down, didn't you?''

''Yes, I did. Andrew got it and rightly so, but the

inequity stayed with me, Kate. I wanted to be able to right wrongs when I saw them.''

''So you left your uncle's law firm because his ethics were questionable.''

''They were. I couldn't stand it another day. My family was surprised, but they have always supported my decision and becoming a prosecutor could be a step toward public office.''

''So in their eyes, it was an admirable change.''

''I wouldn't have cared if it was. It was what I was going to do.''

''Does running for D.A. serve some other kind of need for righting wrongs?''

''No. Not really. It does give me more power and I can prosecute the cases I feel Roth sometimes shies away from because he's afraid he can't win and it'll look bad for the office.''

''You don't care about that.''

''No. I don't give a damn about that. I fight the good fight whatever it takes.''

''What about Danny?''

Jericho turned on the bench and pulled Kate closer, cupping her face. ''I'm an advocate for Mrs. LePlante. She has no one to speak for her. It's my job to get justice for her. If Danny took that woman's life, I'll make sure that he pays for it. It's not up to me to make that decision. A jury of his peers will do that. It's only up to me to present the evidence to them and convince them beyond a shadow of a doubt that he did it.''

''Do you believe that he did it?''

''I don't speculate, Kate. I can only look at the evidence we have now and go forward with that information.''

''But what about Ken Mitchell?''

''I need proof, Kate.''

Kate laid her head on Jericho's chest and sighed. ''Then I'll find it somehow.''

''Legally, Kate.''

She nodded. ''Legally. I promise.''

''There's something I want to ask you.''

Kate raised her head. ''What?''

''I want you to come with me to my first fund-raiser.''

''Are you sure about that? I don't think I'm at the top of the Mitchells' list as most favorite person.''

''I don't give a damn what they think.''

''You should Jericho. They'll give a lot of money to your campaign.''

''I'm small potatoes compared to their backing of Roth for the Senate. I think they expect him to go all the way.''

''All the way?''

''To the presidency.''

''So you really want me at this shindig?''

''Yes, I really want you.''

"Then I'll go." She turned to the piano and began to play chopsticks. "What brought you out here in the middle of the night?"

"I was trying to keep my hands off of you."

"Oh. I guess that's a moot point now since I'm awake."

"Yes. It is."

He grasped her by the waist and lifted her up on the piano, then followed her there. Untying the belt of her robe, he parted the silky folds and spread them across the dark surface of the black wood. She looked like a delicate pink flower on black velvet.

Her hips heaved and bucked when he put his mouth to her. He draped her legs over his shoulders, bracing his hands on the polished top of the piano, he gave her something strong and firm to push against.

With his mouth and tongue he enticed her toward her pleasure, letting it unfold, over and over, blossoming sweeter and hotter.

He wanted her to experience her own vulnerability because she wouldn't allow it. That's why Kate was so afraid of letting go. Feelings scared her and he knew it. She needed to soar free from those limits if ever she was to experience the deepest and most satisfying experience he could give her.

Not yet. She still resisted. Whether it was a failure on his part or hers, he wasn't sure. But he strove to teach her that she was safe with him. That once setting her free and letting her soar, he would be there to catch her when she fell into glorious sensations.

He trapped her hips with his hands and closed his mouth over her sweet bud, sucking, sucking until her slender, strong body flexed and arched. Her hips jerked against his mouth, but he was relentless. She cried out wildly as she exploded, shuddering as waves of pleasure rocked through her.

She slid off the piano, dragging him with her. She shrugged out of her gown and pressed her hands to the curves of his chest, smoothing frantically down his body, undoing his jeans, she yanked them down.

Her mouth was on him in one scalding, hot slide. He jerked hard, his hands coming down onto the keys of the piano making a discordant sound.

Her hot mouth paid no heed to the noise. She sucked at him until he thought he would lose his mind.

She brought him to the brink of explosion and when he realized that was her intent, he grabbed her upper arms and dragged her away.

"Jericho, I want you…"

"No, I want to be inside you."

He swung her up into his arms and kicked his jeans out of his way. In the bedroom, he dropped her on the bed and followed her down.

She yanked him close. "Jericho, please."

He sheathed himself and gave her exactly what she wanted, a deep, thrusting pace that stroked every inch of her swollen, aching sex, to her very depths. He curved over her, the hard, thick muscles of his shoulders firm and tight, his face fixed and focused. Her breath hissed out of her with each hard thrust of his body. All they wanted was the exquisite pace, the driving rhythm. Quick and deep and frantic and insistent, until they both exploded.

He collapsed and draped himself over her, trembling. "My God," he said. "If it's like this with you every time, I'll be dead in a week."

She caressed his face. "But what a way to go."

He grinned at her and then glanced at the clock. "It's almost time to get up and get ready for work. I'll have to leave."

Kate pouted. "Right. You don't have any clothes here. Next time, bring clothes."

"Yes, sir," he said, saluting.

"I mean it," she said, grabbing at his shoulders. "You do want to have a next time, right?"

The tentativeness in her voice tugged at his heart. He'd never want to disappoint this woman; it would be more than he could bear. "Damn right I do. Tonight?"

"Yes," she breathed, pulling his head down for a quick kiss.

Jericho didn't want to leave her for a whole day.

He wanted to stay in bed with her, wrap himself in her sweet presence.

Dangerous, dangerous thoughts. Their bargain was just for the week and it was already half over.

KATE BARELY LOOKED UP when the door to her office opened.

Sienna sauntered in and dropped into a chair opposite the desk. "What's up?"

"I need to ask you about the Phantom Bandit."

"Shoot."

"Did the thief only take personal belongings?"

"Yep."

"But never fenced anything that you know of?"

"No, and the report from Mrs. LePlante's daughter is that there is a diamond bracelet missing from her mother's apartment. A Tiffany original from a high profile boyfriend."

"Did she say who the boyfriend was?"

"No. She didn't know, but she said her mother bragged about him being rich and handsome."

"So, do you have anything new to tell me?"

"Like what?" Kate asked coyly.

"Like how's Jericho this morning."

Kate's eyes narrowed. "Why would you think I know?"

Sienna laughed. "Lana and I came by last night

and saw his car parked out in front of your apartment building.''

''Is that so?''

''You missed out on pizza and beer. But I'm sure your little hands and mouth were too busy to eat or drink. Food, that is. Did you get your souvenir?'' prompted Sienna. ''I'm only asking because you've had a dopey grin on your face since I sat down.'' As she received no reaction from Kate, she stopped and invited, ''Feel free to jump in here with an answer anytime.''

Kate looked at Sienna and sighed. ''No. I forgot to ask him.''

''You forgot? Not a good sign. So is the intense prosecutor as intense in bed?''

''He's very…focused. He plays the piano beautifully.''

''Piano? He played the piano for you?''

''Afterward. He was trying to keep from waking me.''

''Sounds like a good start. Are you going to see him again?''

''Yes. Tonight. He invited me to his first fundraiser.''

''Will the Mitchells be there?''

''Yes, of course. And the D.A., too. Sienna, you investigated Ken Mitchell on the Phantom Bandit case. What did you think of him?''

"Too slick and very smug. He's got a problem with anger."

"Why do you say that?"

"When I was interviewing him, he was getting a manicure. The woman nipped him a little too close to the cuticle and he nearly took her head off."

"Issues with his father."

"That'd be my guess. I think he wants more of the Mitchell pie and daddy doesn't trust him to take over. That's just my overall impression of the guy."

"Do you like him for the Bandit?"

"I do. He was arrested as a juvenile, but his records are sealed. I couldn't gain access."

"Is there some other way you can find out?"

"I could track down the officer who arrested him and have a chat. Mitchell had access to the keys and to the buildings. Whoever got into those apartments gained entry by a key."

"Mrs. LePlante?"

"In her case, it could have been someone she knew. There was no forced entry."

"Could you track down the officer and let me know?"

"Sure." Sienna studied her. "What are you thinking?"

"I want to match up the DNA evidence found at the Bandit thefts to the DNA evidence I found in the shower at the LePlante murder."

"So you thought there was a connection."

"It seems likely."

"But the Bandit hasn't ever murdered before."

"He was surprised. Maybe he reacted."

"I'll keep you posted. Don't forget to ask Jericho for a souvenir. It's time to go to Enrique's and celebrate the end of our dares."

"I'll ask him, don't worry."

"Have fun at the fund-raiser."

Kate held up two tickets to the event. "How about you and A.J. join us?"

"You want to double team Mitchell? Sounds like a good idea to me." She reached out and took the tickets. "I really like seeing A.J. in his whites. Count me in."

Kate sat in her seat for a few more minutes. Then she got up and headed down the hall. Climbing the stairs, she went up into the police station to the psychologist's office.

"Come in."

Kate pushed the door open. "Hi, Dr. Thompson. Do you have a few minutes?"

"Sure, Kate. What can I do for you?"

"I wanted to ask you about kleptomania."

"What about it?"

"Would it be likely that a kleptomaniac caught in the act would kill?"

"Hmm. I would say probably not. Kleptomaniacs don't really have remorse—guilt or shame. They're compelled to steal. Not the answer you wanted?"

"No, not really."

"There's another disorder that's described in the DSM IV that might, though."

"What is that?"

"Addictive/compulsive theft."

"What is the difference?"

"Kleptomaniacs don't steal out of anger or vengeance. They steal because of impulses they can't control. An addictive/compulsive thief does feel shame and guilt after the act," Dr. Thompson explained.

"An individual with this kind of a disorder could possibly kill?"

"Possibly. An addictive/compulsive thief usually steals out of anger. There's usually a lot of tension before the act and a great deal of relief afterward. If he's denied that relief, he might lash out in anger toward the person who interfered."

"Would this type of individual keep the stolen items?"

"Yes, just like a kleptomaniac, an addictive/compulsive thief would keep the items. He may even use some of them."

"Thanks, Dr. Thompson."

"Glad I could be of help."

"MR. ST. JAMES. The D.A. wishes to see you in his office."

The intercom interrupted his thoughts. They

weren't on his next court session or the miles of paperwork on his desk. He wasn't thinking about briefs or depositions or grand jury indictments.

He was thinking about her.

Every supple, beautiful inch of her.

Uncharacteristic, the rational part of his brain admonished. You should be working. He knew he should be working, but he couldn't concentrate. It was like yesterday only worse. Because yesterday had been preceded by the night before when Kate had come to his house and exploded into brilliant sparks right in front of his eyes. Now he knew how those sparks burned and ignited his blood. Now he knew what it was like to immerse himself in Kate.

And he wasn't really sure what to do about it. He never got involved with co-workers. Never. Now here he was entangled in Kate.

''Mr. St. James.''

''I'm coming,'' he said into the intercom and grabbed the camel jacket across the back of his chair and shrugged into it.

He walked out of his office, past the watchful eye of his assistant. ''Are you okay, Mr. St. James?''

''I'm fine, Sandy.''

''You seem awfully distracted.''

''I'm really fine.''

He left his suite of offices and made his way to D.A. Roth's.

He opened the door and stopped dead when he saw Kate sitting in front of the big formidable desk. "Kate," he said softly, unable to disguise his delight in seeing her.

She smiled at him. "Jericho."

D.A. Roth was scowling. "Take a seat, St. James."

Jericho took the chair next to Kate's and cast her a quizzical look. She shrugged.

"It's come to my attention that you, Ms. Quinn, are harassing Ken Mitchell and his father."

Kate launched herself to her feet, her eyes narrowing. "That's a lie. I'm not harassing anyone."

"Sit down, Ms. Quinn. It's also come to my attention that the suspect in custody for the LePlante murder is a personal friend of yours."

"That's right."

"I don't appreciate one of my employees carrying out a personal vendetta against two of the finest citizens of this city just because you're trying to clear your friend. It smacks of a conflict of interest."

"With all due respect, Matt, Kate came to me two nights ago asking to be relieved of this case for that very reason."

"And?"

"I told her that I trusted her to remain professional and do her job, no matter what her feelings were."

"Well, that was poor judgment, Jericho."

Jericho stiffened. In all the time that he'd worked in the D.A.'s office, Matt Roth had given him free rein and relied on him exclusively for his opinion and advice. It shocked him that now he would reprimand him like a sullen teenager. "Not in my opinion, Matt. You used to take my word at face value."

"The Mitchells are very important citizens and I will not have my people harassing them."

"So that's what this is about," Kate said caustically. "Their campaign contributions. No matter that Ken Mitchell could have strangled a woman to death as long as he continues to put money in your coffers."

"That, young lady, is out of line. Can you prove Mitchell killed Mrs. LePlante?"

"No."

"Then…"

"Not yet."

"Perhaps you don't wish to accept that your friend is guilty."

"He didn't kill her. He didn't kill anyone. No amount of evidence will convince me otherwise."

"You're off this case, Ms. Quinn. Turn everything over to Banner."

"I'm more than competent to investigate this case and keep my objectivity."

"Are you? I think you're overestimating your abilities, Ms. Quinn."

"I think she can."

"You're besotted, Jericho. I see the way you two look at each other. Your judgment in this case is off, but I'm giving you a second chance to prove yourself. Prosecute Hamilton to the fullest extent of the law. That's your job."

"Matt, I know my job and Kate knows hers. I think you've made a mistake in removing her."

"It's still my decision. Keep your eye on the ball. And you, Kate. You keep your nose clean or I'll have to take more drastic action. Is that understood?"

"Yes, sir."

"That's all."

They rose and stepped out of his office. "Well that was really fun," Kate said as they were a few feet down the hall. "All over the fact that the Mitchells have money. That's all it's ever about."

11

KATE STOOD AT THE WINDOW overlooking Jericho's property. She had arrived at his house twenty minutes ago. She heard a car drive up and park. Glancing down into the driveway she saw it was Jericho's black Mercedes.

She looked at her watch and saw that they still had plenty of time to get to the fund-raiser. She had arrived at Jericho's long before he had, thanks to Eric's help in clearing her desk. She had made a quick stop at home first, but she hadn't lingered there, packing only a few clothes, toiletries and the items she would need tonight for Jericho's bold seduction.

She looked at her bag in the corner. He was in for a wonderful surprise when they got back tonight. She shivered at the thought of what she wanted to do to him.

She heard the front door open and she walked to the guest room door and opened it. Jericho came down the hall. His eyes lit up when he saw her.

"What are you doing in there? You could have used my room."

"I didn't want to intrude on your privacy without being expressly invited."

"It would have been no problem. It won't take me long to get ready."

He kissed her and when he tried to deepen it, she pulled back. "Oh, no, you'll make us late, Jericho."

"I missed you."

"There will be plenty of time for that tonight."

"Promise."

"Absolutely. Now get to your room."

"You could change in my room."

"Uh, no. That's not a good idea."

"Right. Forty-five minutes."

As soon as she closed the door, she slipped out of her robe. She took the plastic off the electric-blue dress she'd bought for this occasion. Stepping into the slinky fabric, she slipped the straps over her shoulders, turning toward the mirror to lace them over her bare back.

She smoothed the silky material with one hand, turning this way and that in the mirror to check for wrinkles. The dress had tiny straps that left her shoulders bare and most of her back, as well, sheathing her body sleekly. It had an asymmetrical hem with a side slit and mesh inset into the bodice and rib cage that showed just a hint of her skin. Her hair was pulled up in a haphazard knot on her head with cascading curls, and diamond studs glittered at her ears. Taking a deep breath, she left the room to wait for Jericho.

Her reflection mocked, biting her lip not because she was anxious but because she was excited. Kate caught a look at herself and stopped, muttering a curse. She quickly reapplied her lipstick, then put the lid on it and dropped it into her bag.

He didn't keep her waiting long. She heard his footsteps coming toward her and whirled around to face him, her breath stopped in her chest. He was incredibly handsome, and her heart kicked into a faster rhythm at the sight of him. He looked just as handsome now as he did the night of the announcement dinner. Dark, dangerous, and sleek as a panther.

Kate swallowed hard. She wished they were coming home for this evening instead of going out. She wanted to strip the tux off him and have her way with him right now.

She was a little nervous about hobnobbing with the elite of San Diego. Social situations tended to make her nervous. She would much rather sit in a lab and analyze DNA than put on a fancy dress and high heels and try to make conversation. But she wanted to be with Jericho and this was part of his life. Although, unlike her, he fit into the glittering lifestyle and he had no problems with social situations or schmoozing the moneylenders.

His gaze settled on her like a laser beam, making her fidget.

They stared silently at each other, each lost in their own thoughts for long minutes before Kate noticed the missing cuff links.

''Did you forget something?'' she asked, breaking the heavy tension in the air, and he blinked at her before he followed her eyes down to his cuffs.

''I was going to check around for my cuff links. I had them the night of the announcement party but I can't find them,'' he muttered.

''Damn, Andrew gave them to me.''

''He did? They must mean a lot to you.''

''They do.''

''I took them off your shirt when you were sleeping in my office and put them in my jeans' pocket so they wouldn't get lost. I even put them in my robe pocket to give to you, but when we…uh…''

''Made love on the piano?''

''Right. You made me totally forget about them.'' She smiled as she opened her purse and took out the beautiful cuff links. She moved closer and worked each through its buttonhole slowly. The sight of the cuff links made her remember how they'd made love, evoking heated memories. She peeked up at him through her lashes and saw that he was staring down at her hands.

Jericho knew that it wasn't a good idea to touch her, but he couldn't help himself. He reached out and snagged one of her shining curls as it slid over her creamy shoulder.

He played with the silky strands, rubbing them between his fingers. His eyes were drawn to her cleavage peeking out of that racy dress. The soft mounds of her breasts lifted and fell with each breath. If he didn't have five hundred people waiting for him to give a speech after paying five hundred dollars a plate, he'd slip his hand inside that dress and cup her breasts, rolling her hard nipple against his palm.

"Got it," she finally said, running her hands down the front of his shirt. "Ready to go." Her face grew serious as she stared up at him. He was caught in her eyes as if he'd suddenly been immersed in deep blue pools. The air felt electrified as if the molecules reacted to their need and heated. He forgot about the five hundred people, and the five hundred dollars a plate, and the speech. He forgot everything but Kate and the effect she had on him.

"You're beautiful," he whispered, tugging on the curl and reaching out to send his hand over her shoulder down her arm.

''Thank you,'' she managed to say, giving him a distressed look. ''You don't think it's too much?''

''I'd like a little less,'' he said, grinning.

She smacked him on the arm and he laughed.

''That wasn't what I meant, Jericho.''

''I know that, but you looked so serious. I've seen the mayor's wife wear less,'' he said huskily, moving one hand up to cup hers and bring it to his lips.

''Really?''

Jericho pressed a kiss to her palm. He couldn't stay away from her even if he wanted to. She drew him both physically and emotionally. He was feeling things for Kate that would complicate his life. This was a quick fling, a bargain. But his exploration of this woman was becoming too vital to ignore. He should enjoy the time he had with her and worry about the consequences later. ''You take my breath away, Kate,'' he whispered, his face moving closer to hers.

''I'm having a great time, too, Jericho,'' Kate breathed as he hesitated a fraction away from her lips. ''I hope you're not hesitating to kiss me because I'm all dolled up.''

She took the decision out of his hands and pressed her mouth to his, effectively silencing the words he was going to say. She pressed herself against his chest, her hand sliding to the nape of his neck to keep him in place, her mouth hot and sweet against his.

Something more than desire coiled in Jericho's stomach and he slipped his arms around her, trying to be careful of her gown and hair. They kissed each other as if they were saying goodbye, hard and frantic, their tongues joining avidly, before he finally broke away.

He rested his forehead against hers, their breathing labored. "We'd better stop or we'll never leave here," he murmured, touching her mouth regretfully. "I messed up your lipstick."

"You got some on you," she said huskily, her thumb wiping at his bottom lip.

Without any more words they went out the door and Jericho opened the Mercedes door for her as she got in.

He felt closer to her than ever. It made his heart sing, but also made him somewhat worried about how he was going to let her go when she got her souvenir.

THEIR SEATS were at the head table because Jericho had to give his speech later on. Kate tensed when she saw that Ken Mitchell would be seated right next to her.

"Are you okay?" Jericho asked, covering her hand with his.

Kate slid her glance to him. No way would she let on about the conversation she had had with Sienna earlier that day. "No worries," she responded calmly, turning to meet his eyes. His head naturally moved closer to hers, a slight frown furrowing his brow, and she sensed that he wasn't convinced as he glanced at Ken Mitchell. Her next words were the perfect distraction. "The only man who is of any interest to me is you."

The evening progressed and many people took up Jericho's attention. Kate watched Ken Mitchell, trying to act as though she wasn't.

"Good turnout for Jericho," Sienna said, coming up to her.

"Yes. Should add to his campaign coffers nicely."

"Ken seems restless."

"I hope I'm not being too obvious," Kate said. "I've never done a stakeout before."

"You're doing fine," Sienna smiled. "I found out what Mitchell was arrested for."

"What?"

"Shoplifting."

"Interesting."

"I thought so." Sienna eyed the tray of champagne flutes, but didn't partake. "How's it going with Jericho?"

Kate inhaled and let out a dreamy breath. "He's

fabulous. I've got really sticky plans for him to-night.''

"Oh, yeah? What?"

"He doesn't know it, but he's going to be dessert.''

"Mmm, sounds good. You go, girl.''

"A.J. looks good. Is teaching at Coronado agreeing with him?''

"He loves it and the best thing is he's home every night. I had no idea I would fall so deeply in love with him when I first met him. This souvenir business gets damn tricky.''

"Right. Wasn't he supposed to be a one-night stand?''

Sienna laughed. "A.J. is relentless when he wants something. And he wants me, thank God.''

"How are the wedding plans coming along?''

Sienna rolled her eyes. "My mom is really getting into it. You are going to be one of my maids of honor, right?''

"Of course, you have to ask?''

"He's on the move,'' Sienna said softly. The whole while they talked she hadn't lost her concentration on her target.

"He's going over to his father,'' Kate said.

"Looks like this is round two in an argument they started before they got here.''

"Looks like it.''

Kate's gaze was cut off as Jericho walked between her and Ken.

"It's time to eat, Kate," Jericho said.

Dinner passed with nice conversation, but Ken was quiet, giving angry sidelong glances at his father.

Keeping one eye on Ken, Kate said, "Are you nervous about speaking?"

"No. I don't get nervous in front of people."

"That's why you make such a good prosecutor."

"No. I just like to argue," he said.

"I think it's more that you like to prove that you're right."

"Most of the time, I am."

The rest of the meal passed unremarkably.

Kate glanced over at Sienna and she nodded. She was ready.

When Jericho reached the podium and began to speak, Ken Mitchell shifted in his seat. The argument she'd witnessed between him and his father made her wonder about what the psychiatrist had said. Addictive/compulsive theft was usually preceded by a tense moment. She'd describe the interchange between his father and him as not only tense, but very unpleasant. It was obvious that Ken's father neither respected nor trusted his son. That had to sting.

Jericho's words reached her.

"Ladies and gentlemen and members of the bar. I have been asked to speak to you tonight about my role as a prosecutor. I could stand up here and spout that we are the keeper of the flame of both justice and order. I could tell you that the satisfaction of what I do makes it worthwhile. I could tell you many different reasons.

"I could tell you that the public creates a prosecutor and endows him with power through the courts. That a prosecutor can become a leader in developing legislation, proposing constitutional amendments to improve deficiencies in the system, have an interest in community activities, is respected by state and national professional associations, and that participation in advisory board meetings and policy-making groups are a very important part of the job.

"But there is no convincing you unless deep down inside of you there is a passion. This job requires so much of you.

"It hurts.

"It frustrates.

"It takes.

"There are days when I don't even think I could gather enough courage to walk into another courtroom.

"But I do. I'm here to tell you that this job is not about power, not about prestige, definitely not about politics, or even about hard work. This job is about people. First and foremost and forever it's about the victims.

"We are here and we do the job for them.

"Period.

"Because I care about people and care about their rights, I chose prosecution.

"Above all, I am concerned with fairness as much as I am about putting criminals behind bars and can recognize that the two goals are interrelated, not contradictory.

"I have absolute integrity and believe deeply in fair play, use honesty and fairness in dealing with adversaries and the courts, prepare carefully, do not bow to conjecture or leave anything to chance, and never proceed in any case until convinced of the guilt of the accused or the correctness of my position.

"To be a prosecutor demands staunch personal qualities—timeliness, dependability, accuracy, thoughtfulness, decency, personal courage and conviction.

"I will tell you that I *love* this job and somehow the ideals become part of you.

"Keeper of the flame of law and order? May it burn forever.

"Having said all that, I want to remark on my qualifications for the job.''

That was when Ken left the table. Kate waited a couple of beats and met Sienna's eyes.

She rose at the same time Kate did and they soon met up in the lobby of the hotel. Ken was just getting into his Porsche as they burst through the lobby doors. Sienna signaled to the valet and Sienna's car was brought right away.

Sienna took off as soon as the doors closed. "Want to bet he's going to your building?"

"Sounds like a fool's bet to me," Kate replied.

They pulled up to Kate's building as Ken was going through the doors. They rushed out of the car and into the building.

"He's gone upstairs." Sienna lifted up her dress and pulled out her gun. "Nice," Kate said as they ascended the stairs. They crouched and watched as Ken looked around.

"The bastard's at your apartment."

"Yeah, I guess he couldn't resist his compulsion."

They watched as he inserted a master key into the lock and turned the knob and went inside. As soon as the door closed, Kate and Sienna hotfooted it to the door. They waited for fifteen minutes and finally the doorknob jiggled and Ken stepped out.

Sienna put her gun to his head and said firmly, "Looks like you're under arrest, Mr. Phantom Bandit."

KATE STOOD at the observation window while Sienna talked to Ken.

"Why don't we save a lot of time, Ken? Tell me why you killed Mrs. LePlante."

"I didn't kill her!"

"We've found DNA evidence in the bathroom both on glass shards and in the shower."

"So."

"Is that DNA going to match yours?"

"I don't know."

"I think it will."

"I want a lawyer."

Jericho came through the door, shutting it quietly. "What is my little detective doing now?"

"Watching Sienna interrogate the Phantom Bandit."

"Feeling pretty smug, are you?"

She turned to smile at him. "Yes, I am. At least this puts reasonable doubt into not only the jury's mind, but in yours, too."

"Caught him red-handed."

"Sure did. He took a diamond pendant and a pair of my black lace thong underwear."

Jericho looked toward Ken and suddenly Kate was very glad that there was a barrier between him and Jericho.

She touched his arm. "Don't go all macho on me now."

"I'd just like five minutes with him," Jericho said very low. A chill slid down Kate's spine. He turned that inscrutable look on her. "He could have been armed, Kate."

"I'm not a total fool. I took Sienna with me and she was armed. She's really scary when she's in her cop mode."

"I bet."

"So you were right about Ken. What made you follow him tonight?"

"The fact that he never fenced the items was telling. I thought he was a kleptomaniac, but after I talked to Dr. Thompson, I found out that he might be an addictive/compulsive thief. She told me that they tend to react to a tension-filled situation. I watched him and sure enough, he had a run-in with his father. It was a nasty fight. I figured he needed to blow off steam. Now I need your help."

"In what way?"

"Get me a court order for a DNA sample."

"I'll wake up Judge Drury. She likes me."

FORTY-FIVE MINUTES LATER, Kate had her court order. She walked into the interrogation room and presented the court order to Ken's lawyer who had shown up thirty minutes ago.

The man read it. "You'll have to comply, Mr. Mitchell."

Kate took out a swab on a long wooden stick. "Open your mouth, Mr. Mitchell."

"This is all your fault, you bitch."

Ken went to rise, but Jericho was there, placing his palm into the middle of Ken's chest and pushing him forcefully back into his chair. "Touch her and I'll break your arm."

Kate looked at the grim lines of Jericho's face and she realized with a shock that he meant it.

Ken sat in the chair and the anger seemed to drain out of him. He opened his mouth with a sullen look on his face.

Kate swabbed his mouth rich with cells, secured the sample and left the interrogation room. Back in the lab, she got busy breaking the DNA down in the process of DNA testing.

She heated the DNA strands in a glass test tube to ninety-four degrees, separating the molecules completely. Carefully adding primers to combine with the strands of the DNA, she lowered the test tube temperature. Adding a DNA enzyme—poly-merase—Kate prepared the samples to go into a thermal cycler to rebuild a double strand of DNA, effectively duplicating the DNA. The machine would repeat this process over and over in thirty cycles to yield more than one million copies of the DNA.

Close to the end of the process, the lab door

opened and two strong hands settled on her shoulders. Kate would know his scent anywhere. She leaned back into Jericho's chest, moaning softly at the glorious feel of his hands massaging her shoulders.

"How much longer?"

"Almost done with the first step. It'll take at least forty-eight hours to complete the whole process yielding preliminary results," she said wearily.

"Time to go home?"

She looked up at him. He looked as tired as she felt. "You've been in with the D.A.?"

"How did you guess?"

"You have that look."

"He's royally pissed."

"At me?"

"Yes. He said you were removed from the case and he's mad that you went beyond your boundaries."

"I had a hunch and I followed up with it. He should want his investigators to be relentless. Besides, I had a detective with me. The very one working on the Phantom Bandit case."

"I think he's more pissed that you've jeopardized my funding for my campaign than anything else."

"How do you feel about that?"

"The funding?"

"Yes."

''I don't give a damn, Kate. I'm not a politician and I have no patience for it. I think that becoming D.A. would give me a chance to fine-tune our process and allow me to dictate how we prosecute criminals.''

''You think Roth is too soft?''

''I think that he's not as aggressive as I would be.''

She nodded, beginning to wonder if Jericho's association with her would ruin his chances of getting where he wanted to be. She admired his tough attitude and she couldn't be sorry about nailing Ken Mitchell, but getting involved with a co-worker could cause much more trouble for them down the line. Kate cleaned up her work area, made sure the process was working and they left the lab.

12

HE HAD KATE in his bedroom. Finally. She walked in and stood for a moment, taking it in. Had she fantasized about being here just as he had about having her here?

There was a rolltop desk near the French doors to catch the most amount of light. An antique highboy that matched the four-poster bed with intricate scrollwork of birds and fruit carvings. A little ornate for his tastes, but he'd given the decorator free rein in his house. Most of what she'd done, he liked, but this room he felt needed a feminine touch. It was rich in mahogany wood, heavy caramel and red brocade, and echoed with loneliness.

She walked to the bed and curled her hands around one of the four posts. Her fingertips flowing over the carvings.

"This is beautiful, but seems a bit much for you, Jericho."

He smiled at the way she had effortlessly slid into him, already knowing his tastes.

"It is."

She was a seductive vision in her blue dress and black high heels. A choker-tight strand of pearls wrapped around her throat then flowed down to her navel. He wanted to see her in nothing but those pearls.

She left the bed and walked to the desk, peered at the array of pictures over them. Pictures of his friends and family.

''I see,'' she said softly, her hips swishing seductively as she walked. Her bared back looked like creamy silk in the dim glow of his bedside lamp.

''See what?''

''That you like to keep your private life, uh, private.''

''What?''

''There are no pictures in your office, no mementos, but here there are pictures and bits and pieces of your life.'' She ran her hand over his polished desk, the scarlet-painted nails erotic in the half light.

''If you want to know anything about me, all you have to do is ask.''

With her back to him, her eyes still gazing at the pictures, she said, ''I already know so much, but I want more.''

He closed his eyes at the soft, husky tone to her voice. ''Like what?'' he asked.

She turned then and walked up to him, slipping her hands under the tux jacket and pushing it off his shoulders. "Like the tattoo you have down here." Her hand slid down his chest and rested on the bulge of his pants. "I've already been with you twice and didn't get a chance to really see it, even though I was up close the night we made love on the piano."

She pulled his shirt out of the waistband of his trousers and deliberately popped the studs as she pulled the fabric apart. They flew every which way.

Her usually angelic eyes were a deeper, richer blue, swirling with a hunger that sent a shiver of awareness down his spine. A white-hot flame that burned. A hunger that called to his own. A recognition of a common need that could only be fulfilled by him for her, her for him.

He closed his eyes as she splayed her hands against his chest, her palms silky as they ran over his pectoral muscles and down the hard ridges of his abdomen.

"I used to sit in your office and wonder at the hardness beneath your shirt. You have such wonderful broad shoulders." She ran her hands over them, down over the hard bulge of his biceps. "Little did I know that reality would be so much more exciting than fantasy."

"What else did you imagine?"

"Having you completely at my mercy."

"Whoa," he said, closing his eyes at the ripple

of sensation that went through him, sending heat pooling in his groin.

"I used to wonder," she whispered against his ear, "whether you knew how to let a woman lead. All that virile strength and power in my hands made me wet."

"You were wet and aroused sitting there in front of my desk?"

"Yes."

"Why didn't you do something about it?"

"I was inhibited and repressed, just like you said. My friends teased me all the time, but they were right, too. I was Sister Kate."

"And you wanted to change that."

"Yes, desperately. But only with you Jericho."

"Why me?"

"You were so intimidating, so male and seemed way out of my league."

Her hands drifted down to his belt. She unbuckled it, brushing her hands against his waist. She pulled it free of the belt loops and let it fall to the floor.

She unzipped his trousers and pushed them off his hips. Pulling the waistband of his briefs over the pulsating shaft made him moan softly.

Kate's body felt as if it was charged with electricity, currents of awareness and sexual need sizzling between them. This was her night and Jericho would have to succumb. He tried to take charge, his mouth already demanding on hers. Although his hunger made her ravenous to keep that clever mouth on hers, Kate sidestepped his kiss.

"Oh, no. Tonight I'm the one in charge."

Digging deep for control, she placed her hand against the heavy wall of his chest to keep all that male charisma within a manageable distance. His eyes, gleaming with sharp desire, looked like variegated tiger's eyes, light on the edges darkening toward the lustrous center. "You'll have to let go tonight, Jericho. Give yourself over to me. Tonight you're mine to entice."

"Am I?" He grinned.

The smile flashed, stirring her blood, making her sigh and fight against letting him take over. She was one lightweight if she'd let him seduce her with his amazing smile and devastating eyes. She had to be strong, commanding. No shy acquiescence for her tonight.

"I don't think I've ever been this intrigued in my life. Exactly what do you have in store for me?"

"And ruin my surprise. Oh, I don't think so. You'll find this surprise very…delicious," she teased.

"Come on, tell me, Kate."

She danced out of his reach and shook her head. "Nope. And if you keep fooling around, you won't get it at all."

"And I want to get it?"

"Oh, yes. You'll want this very much. Before we go any further, I need to ask you to trust me. In all that I do tonight, I only want your pleasure. Can you do that?"

His permission meant so much to her. She wanted him to trust her implicitly.

He settled his hands on his hips and studied her face. The raging desire in his eyes softened. "Do your best, Kate. I trust you."

"Total control is what I want." She raised her chin, feeling powerful in her demand. But she needed to do this, had to have full control of the vibrant man in front of her. Nothing less would do.

The wicked ideas she had played around with in her mind for years required that he give his assent for her to go forward.

"You're really starting to turn me on in a big way, Kate. Your confidence is extremely sexy."

"Letting me explore my sexuality is your doing." She felt invincible, on the edge of discovery, and she wanted to take that plunge with the man in front of her. "It takes a strong man to be willing to relinquish control."

"And it takes a strong woman to get him to do so. I am your slave."

A triumphant feeling settled in her chest, curving her lips into a self-satisfied smile. "Time for fun and games, then." She put her hand flat against his chest. "Starting now, you cannot touch me without my permission and be assured that I will not always give you permission. You on the other hand, I can explore all night if I wish."

His wicked laugh settled into her pores, permeated her skin, shot heat and pleasure through her. He was by far the baddest man she'd ever met, sure in his masculinity, tough and fair and sexy as hell. She already wanted him to take her, but she pushed that need aside. Another time. Tonight was to prove to herself that Sister Kate was gone.

She showed him her back. "Unlace my dress," she ordered, and soon felt the warmth of his fingers as he untied the ends of the laces, releasing the pressure of the dress against her shoulders and collarbone. She leaned back against him and reached up to twine her arms around his neck. "Take it off."

From his vantage point she was aware that he could see her cleavage and he'd get the full view of her lacy bustier. His breathing increased. She could feel his chest expand and the material slipped off her shoulders, down over her breasts to pool at her waist.

His hands poised to touch her, then he remembered her edict.

"Kate, may I touch you?"

"No. Now push the dress off my hips and let it fall to the floor."

His hands encased her hips, she watched as he cupped her, taking full advantage of her order. She chose this particular dress for the silky texture of the material. Jericho's senses would be heightened by the feel of the material against his palms, make him even more desperate to touch her skin.

As the dress slipped off her waist and over her hips, the glorious slide of material caressed her body all the way to the floor. It was an exquisite sensation to have Jericho undress her like this.

"Kate," he said, his body shaking with the desire she could almost sense in the air.

"No."

He sighed. She moved away from him, bending over to give him the full view of her bottom with only the tiny heart cutout nestled in the small of her back. He groaned and she smiled. Perfect.

She rose and turned. His eyes swept down her body, taking in the bustier, the scrap of black lace at the juncture of her thighs and the garter belt around her waist, supporting the black stockings against her taut calves and thighs.

Dangling the dress from her curled fingers, she held it out to him. "Hang this up. There's a hanger on the bed."

It was a ploy to make him wait, to let the anticipation build; calling attention to the bed also heightened his desire to lay her across it to slake his desire. Need coiled in her groin, but she overcame her sudden desire to strip him and have her way with him.

She walked around to the side of the bed while he hung the dress in his closet. It looked exotic there, like a sapphire-plumed bird among plain dark brown, blue and tan hens. So feminine and delicate surrounded by his masculine clothes.

He turned toward her, the fire in his eyes raging.

''Come here,'' she whispered, running her fingers along the footboard and across the brocade bed-spread. With her other hand she pulled out the pins in her hair so that it came tumbling around her shoulders all the way down her back, past her butt. When she moved her head she gave him a tantaliz-ing peek-a-boo at the black lace heart and her bot-tom.

Jericho growled and she could feel the heat of his body as he came up behind her. She set the pins on the end table and took a brush.

She reached back and handed it to him. ''Brush my hair.''

He took the brush and started at her left temple, dragging it slowly, seductively, through her hair. She shivered and felt his awareness against her back like a lick of flame. He brushed her hair methodically, his fingers grazing her temple. Strong, masculine hands that were very good at holding a woman, stroking, caressing. Every stroke seemed intimate beyond her belief.

"Can I press myself against you?" he asked.

His words were soft and needy. Desire flared in her hot and urgent. "Yes," she replied.

His lower body pressed up against her softly rounded buttocks. His heat scorched her. She could feel the hardness of his arousal press into her, and an aching need tied her stomach in knots, sent a rush of heat over her exposed skin and sparked a fire that began to burn.

He lifted her heavy hair off her left shoulder, pushing the mass aside. The brush stilled.

"Can I kiss your neck?"

"Yes," she replied on barely a breath. Then she felt his lips on the curve of her neck and heat burst through her. Right now everything seemed as it should be. God help her, but she desired him, his touch, his body. His mouth moved to the top of her shoulder and she dipped her shoulder down away from his lips.

She wanted to turn around and throw her arms around his neck, tell him with words and lips that she desired him more than any man in her life.

He went back to her hair.

His fingertips brushed along her scalp, sending

little prickles of heat into her neck as he gathered her hair together. With deft movements, he finished, taking every opportunity to touch her skin all the way down her back. The rogue.

She turned without warning and grabbed at his hips, shoving his buttocks against the edge of the bed. She placed her hand flat in the center of his chest and slid her palm down, her fingers wisping over his rib cage and hard-ridged abdomen. She didn't linger, and he gave a primal groan of pleasure as her fingers pressed against the thick ridge of his erection straining against the tux pants.

His body jerked in response when she stroked him, and it was all she could do not to drag his pants over his hips and put her mouth on him. "Now let's take a good look at this tattoo you've got."

Taking the same route as her palm, her mouth pressed against his chest, openmouthed, her tongue sliding down until she reached the waistband of his pants.

"Kate…"

"No."

"You're killing me."

"Oh, Jericho, we've only just begun."

He groaned at that. She undid the button and zipper of the pants and hooked her thumbs around the black briefs, sliding them over his hips, down his legs and off. Discarding the pants, she went to her knees in front of him. The tattoo was simple, done in black lines in a form of a wishbone. "That is so damn sexy."

She grasped his erection and moved it slightly so she could see better. Jericho was breathing hard, and she was sure he was battling his urge to touch her. While she slowly moved her hand up and down his shaft, she leaned forward and traced the pattern with her tongue.

Jericho swore and she'd never heard him use that word before. A rush of power and awareness sizzled through her.

She rose and stepped away from him. He looked so deliciously handsome standing there in the throes of his desire. She just wanted to stare, but she saw the impatience there, too, and she didn't want to be thrown to the mattress and ravished. She had other plans.

"Remove my shoes," she said softly. He took a deep breath and knelt down. Grasping her ankle in his big hands he removed first one sexy sandal then the other.

"Do you know how to…"

He surged up her body and grasped one of the garters; with a flick of his fingers it was loose. She gasped as he moved around her, easily releasing the other garters. The sleek slide of his cock against her stomach, silken torture.

With both hands she pushed him onto the bed and raised her leg. With deliberate slowness, she slid the silk stocking down her leg and off her foot. Mimicking the motion with her other leg, she said, "Lie back." He did as she asked.

She climbed onto the side of the bed, careful not to straddle him. He looked as if he was so close to the edge of losing it. Taking his wrists in her hands, she tied him to the bed.

Running her palms along the hard slope of his shoulders and down over his chest, she straddled him.

The sight of him bound sent a rush of insidious heat settling in her groin.

She wrapped her arms around his neck and brought his mouth up to hers to give him a carnal, mind-blowing kiss. With just the pressure of her mouth, she coaxed him to part his lips and her tongue slipped inside to mesh with his. Her fingers wove through the hair at the nape of his neck, her breasts compressed against his chest, one slipping out of the bustier, her nipple abrading his hot skin. She moaned against his lips, the carnal mating of their mouths generated enough heat to make them both come apart.

She ripped her mouth free of his and scooted off the bed. He turned his head, his eyes glazed and burning from desire. She'd always wanted to do this. It was a powerful fantasy to strip for him.

She cupped her unclad breast and slid her hand to the peak, twisting her nipple into a hard peak. A low moan slipped up her throat and hummed against her lips.

"Please, Kate, you're so beautiful. I want to be inside you so badly, I'm vibrating."

"Wait, it'll get so much better," she managed a heated whisper, reaching behind her back to unclasp the bustier. As soon as the hook released, her other breast spilled free, the tight points of her nipples jutting toward him as if pleading for his mouth.

"You're the boss tonight."

She got back onto the bed and straddled his hips. The hard heat of his cock scorched her and her hips pulsed a couple of times before she got herself under control. Jericho's face contorted in sensual agony.

He swore again, the word a soft, slow exhalation.

She reached across his chest, thrusting her breasts close to his face, but keeping them just out of reach. She slipped her hand into her bag and pulled out a scarf, silky and soft.

"You are a cruel woman."

He stared into her eyes and saw Kate transformed from the repressed, inhibited woman he'd known to this radiant, sex goddess straddling his body. He'd kept his part of the bargain and she'd kept hers. This night would end their pact.

She leaned forward. "You've helped me to realize my own sexuality, Jericho. The strong, giving, virile man that you are released the passionate woman inside me. I'm no longer afraid. Are you?"

"Of what?"

"Of letting go of all restraints and letting me give you pleasure the way you've given me pleasure."

"I'm not afraid of doing anything with you, Kate."

She smiled, warm and genuine, and placed the blindfold across his eyes.

She reached across him and plugged something into the wall outlet. But with the blindfold on he couldn't see what it was.

Then the soft sweep of something moved across his chest. He realized it was a feather. She wove it over his skin, bringing blood to the surface, making his skin ultra-sensitive, ultra-hot. He gasped when she traced it over his sex and down the insides of his thighs.

"I love that sound, Jericho," she said softly. She reached across him again and then her mouth was against his, sweet with juice from some kind of fruit. He opened his mouth and the taste of the cherry she had in her mouth burst against his tongue. She transferred the fruit to his mouth as he bit down, chewed the luscious fruit and swallowed.

She did the same with a strawberry, a piece of apple and a piece of pineapple.

Each taste was heightened by his blindness and a surprise, first sweet, then tart, then sweet again.

Then she leaned away from him, her breasts brushing his chest, and he wanted his hands free to caress her. He parted his lips to speak and a new taste was placed on his tongue, rich, decadent and creamy. She rubbed his mouth, trailed down over his chin to his breastbone. Chocolate, he identified the exquisite taste. It was warm and melting on his skin and the realization of what she was planning to do with it made him burn with a white-hot blaze of desire.

She removed the blindfold and met his gaze, a suggestive smile on her lips.

"I chose chocolate because your hair and eyes are the sinful color of that sweet treat. I want to taste it from your lips, rub my breasts against you, and lick it clean from your body."

She placed her finger in her mouth and sucked off the small amount that was there. The look of pure bliss on her face made him move restlessly beneath her.

She reached over for more chocolate and dabbed some on his nipples, swirling it around and around his hardening nipples. Bending over, she placed her mouth against him and sucked. The wet heat of her mouth sent rippling sensation arrowing into his groin.

The decadent scent of pure sinful chocolate filled

his senses. She pushed her hot body down his torso, bending over and using her breasts to paint a path of chocolate to his navel.

WITH DELIBERATE LICKS and light bites, she spent time lapping chocolate off his tattoo. This sensual torment was almost more than he could bear. He wished his hands were free so that he could take control of the situation. But he knew that he wouldn't because this was Kate's night.

Her attention switched from his lower stomach to his erection. With hands coated with chocolate, she smoothed her palms up his erection.

He almost came out of his skin he was so sensitized to her, so ready for her it was sweet torture.

Her mouth covered the head of his penis as she licked off the chocolate then proceeded down his shaft to the base and back up again.

Jericho groaned uncontrollably, his hips lifting off the mattress.

"Kate, you're killing me."

She paid him no heed. She took him into her mouth all the way to the back of her throat and took him closer and closer to an orgasm.

"Kate, if you don't…stop."

She ignored him, lost in her own sensuous exploration of his body, caught up in giving him the pleasure she promised him.

When she cupped his balls and pressed her thumb

rhythmically to the base of his cock, he could no longer hold back the hot tide of his release.

The shattering orgasm rushed relentlessly through him until he was spent.

Then Kate, a self-satisfied smirk on her face, climbed back up his body.

She straddled his chest and thrust her chocolate-coated breasts in his face and said. ''Suck my nipples, Jericho, please, I'm so ready for you. I want to feel your mouth on my breasts.''

Jericho needed no other command. He took her nipple into his mouth and sucked hard. Kate cried out and arched into him. She moved her shoulders and swung her other breast into position.

Rearing up, she cupped her own breasts and slid her hand into the nest of curls, moaned when she touched herself.

''Kate, let me.''

She opened her eyes and shifted on him, turning so that his mouth could have access to her soft, swollen flesh.

Her hips began to rock when he sent his tongue against her clit, licking and sucking until she was moving wildly against his mouth.

With a sharp cry, she came, the pulsation of her orgasm sweet against his mouth.

13

"YOU WERE INCREDIBLE to let me have my way with you." She released his wrists from the silky stockings. She brushed her fingertips over his mouth and kissed him. His lips were warm and inviting. Just like the decadent dessert, she couldn't get enough of him.

When she had brought him to orgasm with her mouth, it was as if a door had opened in her and all the restlessness, the recklessness, the wildness had rushed out on a wave of power so all-consuming, she had almost climaxed herself. She felt new and reborn.

He flexed his shoulders and sent his arms around her, holding her to him, his body already alive from the sight of her wild abandon.

She climbed off his chest. "It's shower time, bad boy."

"Me? I'd say that you were a very naughty little girl tonight."

"It's one of my most powerful fantasies. I

couldn't stop thinking about it and I knew that I wanted to do this for you, for me.''

He rose off the bed and moved with her to his gleaming metal-and-marble bathroom.

Kate stopped at the door and just stared. ''This is very, very decadent.''

There was a large shower that took up one corner of the room. And the multihead shower caught her attention. She walked over to the frosted-glass doors, opened them and walked inside.

''Oh.'' She ran her hands over the three shower-heads. ''I've got to get me one of these.''

He laughed and turned on the faucet. Kate jumped back with a screech as the cold water hit her hot skin. She grabbed him in a headlock while he continued to laugh. He adjusted the controls while she tried to find his tickle spot.

They washed each other beneath the spray with soapy hands and kisses. One thing lead to another and Kate found her back up against the warm tiled wall, ruthlessly pinned there by Jericho's hard, muscled body. He'd already sheathed himself during their shower.

She'd had enough slow and teasing for one night. ''Hard and fast…hard and fast, Jericho.''

He slid his hands around her buttocks and lifted her against the tile. Her legs went immediately around his waist.

Kate's back arched against the wall at the feel of his thick, hard cock moving in and out of her. It was too much for her, for them. He pressed her to the wall again, her legs tight around him, and thrust up inside her over and over until they both cried out in tandem.

KATE STOOD IN FRONT of Jericho as she dried off his hard chest with a big fluffy towel.

"Did it hurt?"

"What?" he said, his eyes half closed in pleasure as she moved the towel over his skin.

"The wishbone?"

"I don't remember. I was so wasted that night, I don't think I remembered my own name."

"Does the wishbone symbolize what I think it does?" she asked, leaning against him. He looked delicious with his wet hair slicked off his face, the steam eddying around the bathroom in a fine mist, collecting on the mirror until they were just a blur in its reflected surface.

"You have a wonderfully witty mind, Kate."

She had indulged in her wildest fantasy, but Jericho was real and solid. She traced the tattoo with her finger. "Wish for a bone—er?"

"The guys used to say that girls always wanted me. When I got the tattoo, they picked it out. Thought it was hilariously funny."

"But I'm sure you didn't after you woke up with a major hangover and what I'm sure was a major sore, uh, nether region."

Taking the towel from her hands, he secured it around his waist. Grabbing his robe off the back of the door, he bundled it around her. "You have no idea."

"What do you think the DNA test will reveal tomorrow?" he murmured, pulling her out of the bathroom to the bed.

She rummaged around in her bag and suddenly realized that she'd forgotten something. "I think we'll find that Ken Mitchell was in Mrs. LePlante's apartment the night she was killed. Shoot."

"What?"

"I didn't bring anything to sleep in."

He walked over to his dresser as he picked up the thread of their conversation. "You know his attorney will say that he could have stolen from her at any time. Doesn't necessarily place him in the apartment the night of the murder." He pulled the drawer open and pulled out a faded gray T-shirt with Columbia Law across the front.

He came across the room and handed it to her.

She took off the robe and pulled the T-shirt over her head, her voice muffled for a moment in the fabric. "And you'll say, yes it can, since Mrs. LePlante's Tiffany bracelet was there the day she was killed and was missing after she was murdered.'' She reached into her bag for her blow-dryer.

"You are a clever woman." He drew down the bedspread. "You think Danny's totally innocent." He paused and looked up at her.

She shook her head. "Not exactly. He did hit her with the candlestick, but I'm sure it was in what he would call self-defense," she said, going back into the bathroom and plugging in her blow-dryer. "I think Danny should be cleared and set free, though."

"Probably," he said, coming into the bathroom and taking the blow-dryer and brush out of her hands. "Sounds like he's as innocent as you said he was, but I have to wait for the evidence."

Over the soft whine of the blow-dryer, she said, "I understand. The truth, not to mention the evidence, will set him free."

He sent the brush through her hair, the warmth of the air sending goose bumps along her skin. "You are relentless, Kate. I like that," he said, nuzzling just below her ear, then nibbling on her lobe.

She automatically tilted her head to the side, giving him better access to her neck as he worked at her hair.

"All done," he said, shutting off the instrument and setting it on his vanity.

"Thanks," she said. He stepped closer, aligning

her back to his chest. A muscled arm slid around her waist, and he pulled her body to his.

She rested her head on his shoulder, meeting his eyes in the mirror.

''I wouldn't have missed that experience for anything, Kate.''

''Me, either,'' she said. She wasn't going to admit to herself what she felt for Jericho. He was running for D.A. and she would have to accept the fact that he deserved to win. She couldn't be the person to mess that up for him. The emotions for him twisted in her chest and she turned in his arms, unable to look into his eyes.

It wasn't until much later when Kate lay spooned to his body that she felt vulnerable and panicked, but it had nothing to do with her proximity to Jericho. Physically, she was all his in every way, but it was the raw emotions working their way up to the surface that made her feel so exposed to him. Her throat closed and she swallowed hard as the feelings swamped her. He'd said a week. A week to open her up like a flower coming out into the sun. It'd taken less time and he'd kept his promise. The emotions were alien to her, just too scary and unmanageable. But a bargain, she understood. He'd give her the souvenir and she could prove to her friends once and for all that she wasn't Sister Kate.

Right, her mind took over even as her heart objected. Such feelings of passion wouldn't have lasted anyway. They couldn't have. If they did, she and Jericho would just simply burn out. She didn't want to be around for that fall.

It would be too far.

BRIGHT AND EARLY, even before Jericho woke, Kate got up and dressed for work. She went downstairs and brewed a cup of coffee, looking at two blue jays splashing in Jericho's wonderful marble birdbath. His house was beautiful, decorated very tastefully, but it seemed so…unlived in. That was the word. It needed a woman's touch, she thought. But not hers. She wasn't meant for this kind of life. Simplicity and intellectual pursuits was what Kate understood.

But her heart clamored, *you and Jericho fit so nicely together.* She told that organ to shut up and finished her coffee, leaving enough in the pot for him.

She called a cab and as soon as she walked into the lab, she analyzed Ken Mitchell's DNA sample.

Hours later she compared it to the DNA she'd found in the shower. It matched perfectly.

But when she compared it to the DNA from the shower, Ken's blood and the blood from the glass shards, they didn't match. The blood on the glass shards also didn't match Danny's DNA.

Two things occurred to her.

There had been a third person in the bathroom.

And Ken must have seen him.

14

_____

KATE WALKED UP to Sienna's desk. ''He had to have seen who killed her.''

''Ken?''

''Yes. I just finished my analysis and his DNA doesn't match the blood I found on the shards. I was so sure, but I was wrong. There was a third person in the bathroom.''

''What do you want to do now?''

''I want to ask Ken to tell us the truth. At least about Danny, so he can be cleared.''

''Let's go.''

Fifteen minutes later they were sitting in the interrogation room with Ken and his lawyer. ''Look, I told you I don't have anything else to say.''

''Ken, tell us what happened in the bathroom the night Mrs. LePlante died. It's not going to hurt you. We've already got you for the Phantom Bandit thefts. But what you say can clear Danny.''

''The bitch. She never liked Danny. She was always calling him names. I figured it served her right to take stuff from her, especially since she was so into material things.''

''So you did know her?''

''Yeah, she knew my dad. They were really good friends.''

''Why didn't your father come forward with that information?''

''He didn't want to get involved in the murder.''

''You have a lot of anger toward your father.''

''He thinks that I'm a waste and can't handle picking up the reins to his empire. The truth of the matter is, he won't let me. So, yeah, it causes a lot of anger.''

''That's why you stole?''

''Yes, you were right there. I couldn't seem to help myself.''

''What happened that night?''

''I left the party just like Kate said. It took me maybe fifteen minutes to get to Marie's apartment. I had the master keys that I always took from my dad's office. It was easy. I always replaced them, so he was never the wiser.''

''What happened after you let yourself in?''

''I went to her bedroom and took the bracelet. I heard her come in and scream, 'Oh, no.' Then she got on the phone and called Danny. She must have yelled at him for at least ten minutes about the water on her kitchen floor.''

"Danny came over?"

"Right away. He's a good kid. Anyway, he looks under the sink and tells her that she shoved a box of detergent against the coupling and burst the pipe."

"What happened after that?"

"She goes crazy. I mean, she starts hitting Danny with the end of the mop that she was using to clean up the water."

"What did Danny do?"

"What could he do? He tried to leave. He was very upset, but he never raised his voice. When he got to the living room, she blocked the door and kept hitting him. That's where he got the bruises on his arms."

"Then what?"

"He grabbed the candlestick and hit her in the head. She went down and Danny ran out of the apartment."

"What did Mrs. LePlante do after Danny hit her?"

"She came toward the bathroom. I had to duck inside or she would have seen me. I hid in the shower."

"Did someone else come to the apartment?"

Ken clammed up and looked away from her. "Not when I was there."

"Who are you covering for?"

"No one."

No matter what Sienna did or how she interrogated Ken, he wouldn't say another word. They had no choice but to give up.

Kate left the lockup and went over to the courthouse. She made her way to Jericho's office.

"Is he in, Sandy?"

"Yes, but he's due in court in about fifteen minutes."

"Thanks. I'll keep that in mind." She knocked on his door.

He said, "Come in."

Kate turned the knob and opened the door. "Ken's not the killer."

"Are you sure?"

"Yes. There was someone else in that bathroom, someone who strangled Mrs. LePlante to death, left his blood on the glass shards of the mirror that broke when she struggled."

"A third person?"

"Yes, and I think Ken saw him."

"You want me to offer him a deal."

"Yes, I do."

"I'll have to talk to the D.A. about it."

"Whatever you have to do, Jericho."

He looked down at his watch and back at her. "I've got to get to court, but I'll speak to him right afterward. Okay?"

"Yes, thank you," she said as he shrugged into his suit jacket and picked up his briefcase.

"So did he say anything about Danny?"

"Yes, he wrote a statement that exonerates him. How long do you think it'll take to get him out of jail?"

"The wheels of justice move slow, Kate. Have patience. I'll need to see the statement and talk to Ken, then I'll get the charges dropped."

"Good. I'll tell him the good news."

He stopped outside his office door. "You should be proud of yourself, Kate. This was all you. You saved Danny from a trial and jail."

"I never believed he was guilty. Danny just couldn't have done it."

He sighed. "I've got to go."

She nodded and was almost tempted to follow him and watch him prosecute his case. He was fascinating to watch, but she had too much to do in the lab and she really wanted to tell Danny that he'd been cleared of the charges.

It took Kate most of the day to get to Danny's cell. She was called out to a crime scene shortly after she got back to the lab. Then there was the autopsy to attend and the cataloging of the evidence. Finally, she had a few minutes to speak to Danny.

As Kate made her way to Danny's cell, someone called her name.

"Ms. Quinn."

It was Ken Mitchell's voice. She turned toward the cell. "Yes."

"I didn't want to say anything in the interrogation room because I was scared."

"Scared of what?"

"You don't understand. You have to promise to protect me if I tell you who I saw."

"Of course."

"I want to meet with Jericho. I'll tell him who I saw and him only."

"You don't trust me?"

"No, it's not that. If I tell and he finds out, he'll kill you. I'm trying to protect you."

"That's admirable, but unnecessary."

"You don't know who you're dealing with. I'll only speak to Jericho."

"All right. I'll tell him." Kate mused about what Ken had to say all the way to Danny's cell. She would see Jericho as soon as she finished talking to Danny.

BACK AT THE COURTHOUSE, Kate ran into Jericho coming out of his office.

"Hey, I was just going to talk to Roth. What's up?"

"When I went to Danny's cell, Ken stopped me and told me that he did see someone that night, but he will only talk to you. Do you think you could go over there tonight?''

''Sure. Let me finish up with Roth and then I have a meeting with a witness. I'll go over after that.''

''Thanks very much.''

''You can show me your appreciation tonight.''

''Call me when you're finished with Ken and we can grab a bite to eat together.''

He nodded as he left her, hurrying for the elevator.

Kate went back to the lab and started to work. She didn't notice the lab clear out as people went home for the day.

She continued to work until her cell phone rang. ''Hello?''

''Kate,'' Jericho said.

''Great, you talked to Ken. What did he tell you?''

''He didn't tell me anything. When he wasn't in his cell, the guards looked for him. He was found in the shower, stabbed.''

''Oh, my God! Is he dead?''

''No, but he lost a lot of blood. They've taken him to the hospital. That's where I am now. I was hoping he'd wake up in the ambulance, but no dice. The doctor isn't sure he'll make it through surgery.''

''Do they have any idea who did this?''

''No. No one saw anything and Ken really hasn't

been here long enough to make enemies. But he was stabbed with a homemade shank.''

"This is terrible. What are you going to do now?''

"I think I'll hang around here. If he comes out of surgery, I might get a name.''

"Okay. I'll close up here and head on over.''

Kate hung up the phone and prepared to clean up her work area and store the evidence she'd been working on. She heard the door open to the lab, but didn't turn around. A heavy blow to the back of her head knocked her down to the ground, but before she lost consciousness, she saw a pair of highly polished shoes go into the evidence area. Then blackness stole over her like a dark shroud.

ACRID SMOKE FILLED her nose. Kate awoke with a ferocious headache. She rolled over to the phone and hauled herself up. Reaching out, she grabbed the receiver and dialed 9-1-1. She weaved her way over to the fire alarm and pulled it.

Moments after, the sprinkler system kicked in and soaked her to the skin. She collapsed into a heap on the floor. She heard the sirens get closer and then booted feet on the stairs. Smoke was heavy in the room, but every time Kate tried to move, her head would spin. "Kate!" Sean said, bending down to her. "What happened?"

"Someone hit me. I think they started a fire in the evidence room."

He knelt down and gathered her into his arms and rose. She clung to his neck, her head spinning and bringing her close to the black maw.

When she hit the fresh outside air, she started to cough, but a paramedic was there with an oxygen mask and put it over her nose.

"Kate! Oh, my God, what happened?" Sienna said to Sean.

"Someone hit her and started a fire in the lab. It's a good thing that fire didn't reach the chemicals stored there or there would have been one hell of an explosion."

Kate registered that information as she breathed deeply.

"I'm going with her," Sienna said, flashing her badge. She climbed inside the ambulance and grasped Kate's hand.

"Is she okay?" Sean asked the paramedic.

"Yeah, she's stable. Nasty blow to the head and probably a concussion."

"Who did this to you, Kate?"

"Don't know." Her words were muffled behind the mask.

The ride was quick and when they pulled up at the ER door, Jericho was there to greet the ambulance.

"Katie," he said softly, grasping her hand, demanding information from the paramedic. The paramedic answered his rapid-fire questions.

They wheeled her toward an examining room and a nurse said, "You'll have to let go of her, sir."

Jericho reluctantly did so. "I'll see you soon."

Kate nodded.

As soon as they closed the examining room door, Jericho called the D.A. on his cell phone. Matt would need to know what had happened tonight both with Ken Mitchell and the fire at the lab.

Kate had looked so pale and Jericho wished he could get his hands around the neck of the person who had put her in danger.

Lana, dressed in a San Diego Fire Department T-shirt came slamming through the ER doors. Running to the desk, she asked about Kate.

"Kate Quinn. Where is she? I was told she was brought to this hospital.

"Excuse me," he said, "Remember me? I'm Jericho St. James."

Lana turned toward him and stared for a moment. Coming to some kind of conclusion, she reached out her hand. "Is Kate here?"

"They have her in an examining room," he said, running his hands through his hair. "They won't tell me anything."

"Where?"

"Number Two."

Lana brushed past him and headed toward the door. She grasped the knob and twisted it. Jericho followed her as Lana went into the room.

Kate was sitting up and a doctor was looking into her eyes.

"What are you people doing in here?"

"Since we can't get any information from anyone else, we decided to find out for ourselves." Lana came over and grasped Kate's hand. "Are you okay?"

"I'm fine. Just a slight concussion, a really bad headache and a little smoke inhalation."

"I…we were very worried about you," Lana said, indicating Jericho standing close to the door, eyeing her with his heart in his eyes.

The doctor caught Kate's attention and gave her instructions about what she had to do. Two days of bed rest, pain reliever for the headache and an ointment for the contusion.

"Thank you."

He left the examining room and Jericho came forward. Lana moved around the table to make room for him. "Are you sure you're all right?"

"Yes," she said, grabbing his hand and squeezing. "I'm fine, really."

Kate turned to Lana. "It was arson, someone set the fire."

"I know. I've already gathered evidence."

"What's destroyed?"

"The evidence locker with the LePlante stuff."

"All of it."

"Except the glass shards. They melted."

"What's this about the LePlante evidence," Matt Roth said as he stepped into the room.

"It's been destroyed," Lana said.

Kate watched as the D.A. walked toward her. Her eyes going to his feet as he stumbled into a stool. Those shoes. They looked familiar…. He reached her and grasped her hand. She looked down and that was when she saw them. The small wounds on either side of his hands. The shoes…the cuts on the hands. Oh God, it was Roth who had started the fire. Roth who had killed Mrs. LePlante.

She closed her eyes, Jericho's arms and hands reached out to comfort her. Her head was spinning, the terrible shock of realizing that the D.A., the man she'd worked for since she started in forensic science, was a murderer.

She leaned into Jericho and buried her face in his jacket. To think she had admired the man. It made her sick to think he was capable of killing. And, oh, God, he must have been the one who'd stabbed Ken.

"Sounds like all is lost in this case. We have one suspect who's retarded, another in a hospital bed. Now all the evidence has been destroyed."

As she leaned against Jericho, she registered Roth's words. She jerked up and met Roth's eyes. "Not all the evidence," she said firmly.

Roth's eyes narrowed and uncertainty flashed there. Good, let him squirm. "What are you saying?"

"Lana just told me that the glass shards have melted. There will still be DNA evidence that I can extract from them. We still have hope."

"That's good news," he said, but not with conviction.

"If I could get back to the lab...."

"No, Kate. You heard the doctor. You have to rest."

"It wouldn't take long to extract the evidence, Jericho. It's important to preserve it."

"Jericho, let her go to the lab. If it's that important," Roth said, giving Kate a sidelong look that sent chills down her spine.

"Report what you find to me. I'm happy to see you safe," he said before he left.

The minute that Roth left, Kate got off the table and went to the door to peer out. Jericho and Lana exchanged looks.

"What are you doing?"

"Making sure he's gone."

"Roth?"

"Yes. He killed Mrs. LePlante."

Lana and Jericho looked at each other again. Jericho came over. "I think it's time for you to get home, soak in a warm bath and get that bed rest the doctor prescribed."

"No, listen to me. When I got hit, a man walked by me. He had on these shiny shoes. I'm telling you it was Roth. He also had cuts on his hands from the glass shards. I know it was him. I have to get back to the lab."

"To analyze the evidence?"

"There is no evidence to analyze. The fire destroyed all the biological evidence on those glass shards."

"But you told Roth that evidence could be extracted."

"I lied, Lana, so that he will come back to the lab to silence me. Then Sienna can take him into custody."

"THERE'S NO WAY you're going to act as bait," Sienna said.

"It's the only way," Kate cried. "Wire me. Come on, we don't have a whole lot of time. He might get suspicious. Do you want a murderer to escape?"

Sienna looked at Jericho. "What do you think?"

"I can't believe that you're even asking me when you've known Kate just as long as I have."

"Right." Sienna went to the door. "Mike, would you get me a wire?"

"The minute he confesses, I'm moving in," Sienna said as she taped the wire around Kate's waist and fastened the microphone to her shirt.

"That's fine with me."

Sienna, Jericho, and Lana hid in Kate's office while Kate went to the undamaged part of the lab and pretended to extract the DNA evidence from the lump that had once been the shards of glass from Mrs. LePlante's mirror.

When she heard the scuff of a heel on the floor, she whirled around. "D.A. Roth, you scared me," Kate said, hopefully loud enough for Sienna to hear.

"My apologies," he said softly, and pulled out a wicked-looking gun. "Give me the glass shards."

"Why would you want them and why pull a gun on me?"

"I think you know, Ms. Quinn."

"Know what?"

"That I was the one who strangled Marie Le-Plante."

"But why?"

"She was going to ruin my bid for governor. She was going to break the news to the press that I was having an affair with her. I couldn't let her do it. Carrie would have left me and my reputation would be in tatters. My damn platform was family values for Christ's sake. Now give me the damn glass shards.''

''It won't do you any good.''

''Why is that?''

''There is no evidence for me to extract.''

''What? You…''

Sienna burst out of her office and said, ''Freeze, Roth.''

Roth whirled around, swearing viciously, but he had no choice but to relinquish the gun. As soon as he did, Jericho hauled back his fist and hit him flush in the face, knocking him to the ground.

''That's for Kate,'' was all he said.

KATE SAT on Jericho's bed with a bucket of ice. She took Jericho's hand and put it into the frosty cubes.

''Damn that's cold.''

She looked up at him. ''Thanks for punching out Roth, but there was no need.''

''Yes, there was,'' he growled.

She was silent for a moment. ''You're a good man. You'll make a good D.A., Jericho.''

''This is starting to sound like goodbye.''

''You fulfilled your half of the bargain and we both agreed that fooling around with your employee while being a D.D.A. was pushing it, but fooling around with an employee when you're the D.A. wouldn't be a good idea.''

He sighed. "That's right I did, but, Kate…"

She put her hands over his lips. "No. It's the way it has to be. After this terrible scandal, the D.A.'s office will have to redeem itself. It would be bad for your reputation."

"You fulfilled your half of the bargain, too, Kate, so that means you get your souvenir."

He reached over to the nightstand and picked up the cuff links.

"Jericho, no. They mean too much to you."

He took her hand, opened her fingers and placed them on her palm. Then he rolled her hand closed. "Take them, Kate. I really want you to have them. They have my initials on them, a good way to prove you slept with me."

She cupped his face. "And it was so very wonderful. You woke up the passionate woman in me. I feel that, finally, I can embrace that part of myself."

"Good, it was a pleasure, literally."

She wrapped her arms around his neck and held him tight. "I'll never forget what we shared," she said softly against his ear.

"And I'll never forget you, Kate."

She picked up her things, clutching the cuff links in her hand until they pressed hard against her flesh. "See you at work."

"Right."

She walked out of his room, out of his house, and out of his life.

It wasn't until she was safely ensconced in her apartment and seated at the piano, slowly playing chopsticks, that she let the tears fall.

It was better this way. These intense emotions were chaotic and unpredictable, and way too overwhelming. She'd find a nice quiet man to settle down with, one who didn't have sinfully dark chocolate eyes and hair, and a mouth that could kiss her into a coma.

15

KATE TUCKED the second cuff link into the button-hole of the white Oxford shirt she wore. For a moment she looked down at the swirls of Jericho's initials and let herself miss him. Reaching over, she shimmied into the tight black leather pants and pulled them up over a black lace thong, zipping the front. Grabbing a pair of strappy three-inch sandals, she slipped her feet into them and buckled the straps. She turned to look into the full-length mirror.

Goodbye, Sister Kate.

Her new, short and sophisticated hairstyle made her feel light and free. She'd shorn her hair *and* her old way of being. Her eyes were lined in a dark brown, a deep mocha color on her lids. She'd even swept a couple coats of mascara on her lashes. Color bloomed in her cheeks and, as the last step, she applied a dark red to her lips.

Hello Daring Kate.

She was ready for Enrique's and the souvenir meeting of the Women Who Dare.

Jericho had done what he promised. He'd awakened the hot, passionate woman she had trapped inside. The only problem was that the hot, passionate woman wanted Jericho. Only Jericho.

And this daring woman was going to go get him.

It had been ten days since the fire and arrest of D.A. Roth. His indictment a day later had been splashed across the headlines. Her name and her part in the arrest had been documented in the numerous articles and on the major news channels. She'd received six job offers: five from independent labs and one from the FBI. She decided to take the FBI job.

It would expose her to many different cases.

It would challenge her.

It was a lot more money.

And, if she was no longer Jericho's co-worker...

She smiled as she looked at the cuff links one more time. She loved him. She was miserable without him. Switching jobs was the logical choice. He would never have suggested that to her. That's the kind of man he was, but with the offer of a lucrative job, there was no reason she shouldn't take it. The FBI even offered to pay for her to get her Ph.D. in forensic science to sweeten the deal.

The best part was that she'd be in a San Diego based lab and wouldn't have to relocate.

Kate grabbed her purse and her keys and went bouncing down the stairs feeling happy-go-lucky.

"Hi, Miss Kate."

"Hi, Danny. How are you doing?"

"I'm okay thanks to you. You're a good friend."

"You are, too, Danny. I'll see you Sunday morning, right?"

"Right." He smiled. "Cartoons."

Danny Hamilton had been released the same day Roth had been arrested. She'd found out that Jericho had seen to it personally. She knew he'd done it for her.

Ken Mitchell had survived the stabbing, had fingered Roth and was more than willing to testify to both Marie LePlante's murder and his own attempted murder. In return, he would have all charges dropped against him and he'd be required to seek counseling.

Ken's father didn't pull his support as Kate feared, but told Jericho that he was impressed with a man who knew how to keep his own house in order and would continue to back him one hundred percent.

But Jericho had declined his support. He didn't want to accept money from the father of a man he'd dropped the charges for. It didn't seem right to Jericho even if his campaign suffered. But once the news spread about Roth and the part Jericho had played in the arrest, money began to pour in.

Kate pushed open the front door and stopped on the sidewalk just to look at the big present she'd given herself. The mechanic had told her that her clunker just wouldn't make it. So, after her breakup with Jericho, she'd gone out and bought herself a cherry-red Mustang convertible.

"Va-va-va-voom," she said, and a laugh escaped her.

The transformation was complete.

She got into the car and gunned the engine just for the fun of it. Reaching over, she pushed in the CD and a rich voice started singing "Mustang Sally." Kate put the car in gear and pulled out of the space singing at the top of her lungs.

Even though she was running late, she drove straight to Jericho's house. She rang the bell and knocked, but there was no answer. Damn, she must have missed him. The only thing to do was go to Enrique's. She'd catch him tomorrow.

She got back in her car, cranked the music and headed downtown.

When she walked into the club, Sienna was seated at their usual table and so was Lana. A.J. Camacho and Sean O'Neill rounded out the party.

Kate came walking up to the table and she received several whistles, many stares, and a few double takes. She laughed, shaking her hair back.

"Whoa," Sienna said. "Is that you, Kate?"

Lana was speechless and Kate bent over and

chucked her chin to get her friend to close her mouth. "That's a first, Lana, you speechless."

"That's a feat," Sean said, and got an elbow in the ribs for his effort.

Kate laughed and sat down.

After ordering a Sex on the Beach, Kate was about to suggest revealing their souvenirs when all four of her friends' eyes were suddenly riveted to the door.

"What?"

"Don't look now, but I think someone's coming over here and he's looking right at you."

"Well, he can forget it," she said, turning her head as she rose. "The only man I want is—" She came face to face with the man wearing a sinfully tight black silk T-shirt, skin-hugging jeans and a pair of cowboy boots. She butted right up to his chest. The air rushed out of her lungs as she breathed his name. "…Jericho."

His eyes traveled down her body and back up. "Kate, son of a…you look amazing. You cut your hair." His fingers threaded through the soft locks and he smiled. "I like it."

She wrapped her arms around his neck. "I take it you didn't come here to tell me how I looked."

"No." He spied the keys on the table with the Mustang emblem. A grin spread across his face. "The red Mustang is yours?"

"That's right."

"I hope I can keep up with you."

"You can try, mister." She waited a beat. "So, is that all you wanted, to see me and my new wheels?"

"No. I'm withdrawing from the D.A. race."

"What? Jericho, you can't."

"I can get my old job back at my uncle's firm."

"Jericho, you hated that job."

"It's less torturous than the alternative."

"Which is?"

"Living without you. I simply can't."

She kissed him right in front of everyone, deeply, passionately. When she broke free, she cupped his face. "You won't have to quit. I am."

"Kate, no."

"Don't worry. It's a very good job. It's with the FBI."

"In Washington?"

"No. Here in their San Diego lab."

"Are you sure?"

"Positive, because, you see, I simply can't live without you either. I love you, Jericho."

"I love you, Kate."

"Now that that's settled, will you two sit down so that we can call this meeting to order?"

Sienna picked up her drink and turned to A.J. "To A. J. Camacho who brought me out of the dark and into the light. Tough, tender and giving, I thank you for this trident pin that symbolizes the honor of the Navy SEALs. I'll wear it proudly.'' She clinked her glass with her friends and drank as her diamond glittered in the overhead lights.

Lana picked up her drink and turned to Sean. ''To Sean Ryan O'Neill, who taught me my heart's desire. Adventurous, bold and caring, I thank you for this medal that was given to you for your valor. I'll wear it proudly.'' She tapped her glass with Sienna and Kate and they drank.

Kate picked up her glass and turned to Jericho. ''To Jericho St. James, who gave me his fire to ignite my own flame. Honest, relentless and generous, I thank you for these cuff links that show your steadfast sense of justice. I'll wear them proudly.''

Hours later after the camaraderie, the drinking and the dancing, Kate drove Jericho to her apartment in her red-hot Mustang, while A.J. volunteered to drive Jericho's car back to his house for safekeeping.

When Kate and Jericho got out of the car, they kissed on the sidewalk, in the lobby, climbing the stairs, and while she put her key in the lock. They kissed and took off articles of clothing as they made their way to Kate's bedroom. Tumbling into Kate's bed, she sank into Jericho and endeavored to show him how wild and daring she had become.

It was early the next morning when they heard knocking on the door.

Jericho stumbled out of bed and pulled on his jeans while Kate shrugged into her robe. He opened the door and she heard Danny's voice.

"Hi, Mr. St. James. Tell Kate it's cartoon time."

She heard the crackling of the Sunday paper and it warmed her heart when she heard Jericho say, "Come on in, Danny. You can make the coffee."

He walked into her room and shut the bedroom door. "Is this a Sunday ritual?"

"I'm afraid so."

He walked over and gathered her into his arms and buried his face in her neck. "Cartoons?"

"Comics really, but Danny likes to look at the pictures."

"So there's a soft side to my wild woman."

She cupped his jaw and said, "Look who's talking, Mister Softy."

He shrugged. "As you said last night, I can be generous. I know that you love me and we have a lifetime. I can give Danny Sunday mornings."

"Ah, me, being daring and bold does have its rewards."

"Great sex?"

"There's that, but I was talking about a man I love more than anything."

"More than chocolate?"

She laughed and gave him a ribald look. "Actually, I can have you and chocolate, too."

"You already have."

"You know what they say about chocolate and women. We just can't get enough."

"I can't wait," he said huskily as he met her mouth and they began the first step in their very own happily-ever-after.

* * *

Look out for Karen Anders' new title
Manhandling, *available in July 2005, only from*
Mills & Boon Blaze.

0405/21

MILLS & BOON®

Live the emotion

Sensual romance™

THE BEST MAN IN TEXAS
by Kristine Rolofson

A rugged male and an adorable baby—*irresistible!*

Delia Drummond is reinventing herself and looking for some sexy fun with Joe Brown over a long, hot summer. She's got nothing to lose…

Also available in May:

SEDUCE ME by Jill Shalvis
(HEAT)

WHEN THE LIGHTS GO OUT… by Barbara Daly
(THE WRONG BED)

UNDERNEATH IT ALL by Nancy Warren

Don't miss out…

On sale 6th May 2005

PENNY JORDAN

Sweet Seduction

From lust…to love

On sale 1st April 2005

Available at most branches of WHSmith, Tesco, ASDA, Martins, Borders, Eason, Sainsbury's and all good paperback bookshops.

MIRA®
An international collection of bestselling authors

EVER AFTER
by Fiona Hood-Stewart

**"An enthralling page turner—
not to be missed." —***New York Times*
bestselling author Joan Johnston

**She belongs to a world of wealth,
politics and social climbing. But
now Elm must break away to find
happily ever after...**

Elm MacBride can no longer sit back and
watch her corrupt and deceitful husband's
ascent to power and his final betrayal sends her
fleeing to Switzerland where she meets
Irishman Johnny Graney. When her husband's
actions threaten to destroy her, Johnny must
save not only their love but Elm's life...

ISBN 07783 2078 2

Published 15th April 2005

2 FREE

BOOKS AND A SURPRISE GIFT!

We would like to take this opportunity to thank you for reading this Mills & Boon® book by offering you the chance to take TWO more specially selected titles from the Blaze™ series absolutely FREE! We're also making this offer to introduce you to the benefits of the Reader Service™—

- ★ **FREE home delivery**
- ★ **FREE gifts and competitions**
- ★ **FREE monthly Newsletter**
- ★ **Exclusive Reader Service offers**
- ★ **Books available before they're in the shops**

Accepting these FREE books and gift places you under no obligation to buy, you may cancel at any time, even after receiving your free shipment. Simply complete your details below and return the entire page to the address below. You don't even need a stamp!

YES! Please send me 2 free Blaze books and a surprise gift. I understand that unless you hear from me, I will receive 4 superb new titles every month for just £3.05 each, postage and packing free. I am under no obligation to purchase any books and may cancel my subscription at any time. The free books and gift will be mine to keep in any case.

K5ZED

Ms/Mrs/Miss/Mr ....Initials ....

BLOCK CAPITALS PLEASE

Surname ....

Address ....

....

....Postcode.................................

Send this whole page to:
UK: FREEPOST CN81, Croydon, CR9 3WZ